Juneau Black

Shady Hollow

Juneau Black is the pen name of authors Jocelyn Cole and Sharon Nagel. They share a love of excellent bookshops, fine cheeses, and a good murder (in fictional form only). Though they are two separate people, if you ask either one a question about her childhood, you are likely to get the same answer. This is a little unnerving for any number of reasons.

ALSO BY JUNEAU BLACK

Shady Hollow

Shady Hollow

A SHADY HOLLOW MYSTERY

Juneau Black

VINTAGE CRIME / BLACK LIZARD
Vintage Books
A Division of Penguin Random House LLC
New York

FIRST VINTAGE CRIME/BLACK LIZARD EDITION,
JANUARY 2022

Library of Congress Cataloging-in-Publication Data
Name: Black, Juneau, author.
Title: Shady Hollow / Juneau Black.
Description: First edition. | New York : Vintage Crime/Black Lizard, 2022. |
Series: The Shady Hollow mystery series ; 1.
Identifiers: LCCN 2021032465 (print) | LCCN 2021032466 (ebook)
Subjects: GSAFD: Animal fiction. | Detective and mystery fiction. |
Mystery fiction.
Classification: LCC PS3602.L293 S53 2022 (print) |
LCC PS3602.L293 (ebook) | DDC 813/.6—dc23
LC record available at https://lccn.loc.gov/2021032465
LC ebook record available at https://lccn.loc.gov/2021032466

Vintage Crime/Black Lizard Trade Paperback ISBN: 978-0-593-31571-2
eBook ISBN: 978-0-593-46627-8

Book design by Christopher M. Zucker

www.blacklizardcrime.com

Printed in the United States of America
10 9 8 7

Author's Note

Shady Hollow is a tale of woodland creatures, and from time to time the contemplative reader may pause to wonder precisely *how* a town functions with foxes and rabbits as tenants of the same building, or how a mouse and a moose can chat eye to eye. Keep in mind, gentle reader, that this is a work of fiction. The characters' resemblances to real creatures, alive or cruelly murdered, is incidental indeed. For those who feel compelled to resolve this issue before continuing with the story, you may wish to think of the characters merely as humans with particularly animalistic traits . . . in other words, just like you and me.

With that guidance, welcome to Shady Hollow.

Cast of Characters

Gladys Honeysuckle: *As the town gossip and busybody, there's nothing Gladys doesn't know. She was the one to find the body and sound the alarm. But perhaps she already knew where to look . . .*

Otto Sumpf: *The grouchy, taciturn toad of Shady Hollow. Not many folks admit to liking Otto. The better question is who hates him.*

Vera Vixen: *This cunning, foxy reporter has a nose for trouble and a desire to find out the truth. Can she trust anyone around her?*

BW Stone: *The cigar-chomping skunk of an editor of the Shady Hollow Herald. BW ("Everything in black and white!") loves a good headline. Would he kill to create one?*

Lenore Lee: *A dark-as-night raven who opened the town's bookshop, Nevermore Books, and has a penchant for mysteries. If anyone is an expert on murder, it's Lenore.*

Joe: *This genial giant of a moose runs the coffee shop, the local gathering spot. If gossip is spoken, Joe has heard it. Maybe he heard too much.*

Chief Theodore Meade: *Bears make excellent law enforcers: big, brawny, and belligerent. But Chief Meade seems singularly uninterested in solving crime when he could be fishing. Is that fishy?*

Deputy Orville Braun: *This large brown bear is the harderworking half of the Shady Hollow constabulary. He works by the book. But his book has half the pages ripped out.*

Ruby Ewing: *There's none more friendly and forgiving than Ruby. But Ruby has her share of scandals, too . . .*

Reginald von Beaverpelt: *This wealthy industrialist more or less rules Shady Hollow, but not his own family—there is domestic strife with his wife and daughters. And is the sawmill as secure as it seems?*

Howard Chitters: *As the timid accountant for the sawmill, Chitters accepts Reginald's hoity-toity manner and casual verbal abuse. But does he know something about the sawmill's finances that no one else does?*

Anastasia and Esmeralda von Beaverpelt: *The daughters of the town's richest family are happy to shop and gossip, as long as their family secrets stay hidden.*

Edith von Beaverpelt: *Rumor has it that socialite Edith is the real power behind the gnawed-wood throne. Control the purse strings, and everyone listens . . .*

Lefty: *The small-time criminal about town, this masked raccoon lives in the shadiest part of Shady Hollow. But surely he wouldn't cover up for someone else's crime . . . unless there was a big payoff.*

Ambrosius Heidegger: *Professor of philosophy and general know-it-all. The owl is the smartest creature in the forest, and never lets anyone forget it. But is he too smart for his own good?*

Sun Li: *He runs the Bamboo Patch, serving vegetarian dishes to die for. But his past and his identity are a mystery.*

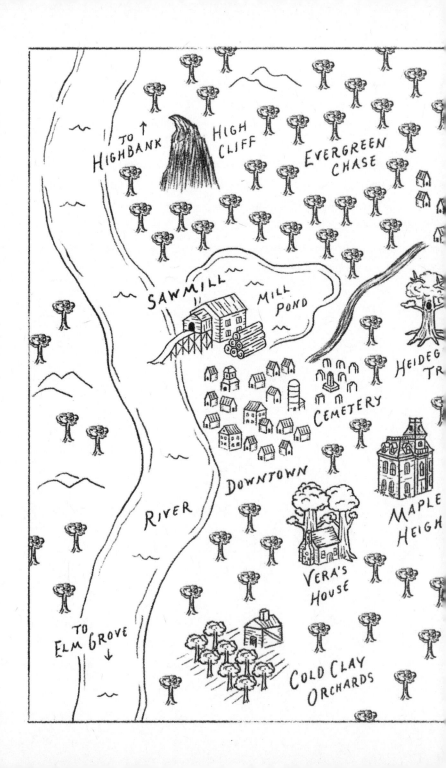

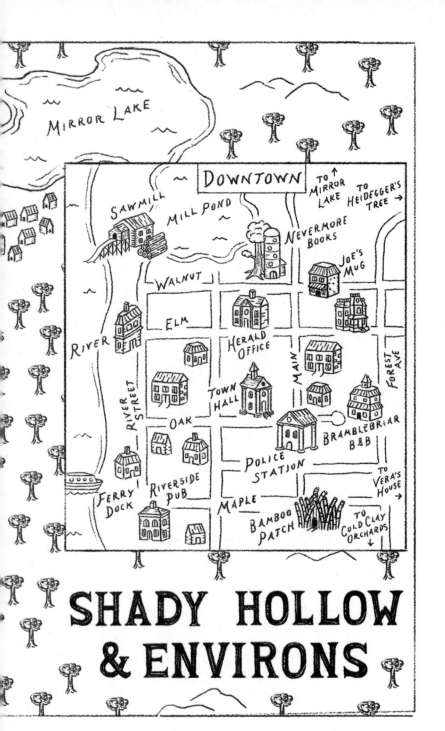

Shady Hollow

Prologue

U p in the far north, away from everything you know and dream about, lies a small village called Shady Hollow. There are many settlements in the woods, far from the cities and the bustling world. Shady Hollow is only one such community, where woodland creatures of all types and temperaments, from the tiny mouse to the mighty moose, live together in a successful and mostly peaceful society.

What does such a place look like? you wonder. First of all, a beautiful river winds through the town. Burbling cheerfully in the summer months, the river slows to a statelier pace in autumn. It freezes over in winter, and the residents of Shady Hollow host skating parties and build snow critters all along the banks. Even the creatures prone to hibernation cannot resist the lure of such icy enchantments in this place! And in spring, the river rushes back to life, nearly overflowing its banks after swelling with snowmelt and seasonal rains.

The river rushes past the sawmill, past the piers, past the town. But in one spot it feeds a millpond, a quiet sort of place where a beast might find solitude . . . if it takes care not to run into Otto Sumpf, that is. Otto, a cranky toad, lives alone in the swampiest bit of the pond, in a mud hut surrounded by tall grasses and cattails. He patrols the shore as if it were his sworn duty and prides himself on starting arguments on any subject.

One of his very favorite topics juts up at the other end of the pond. The Von Beaverpelt Sawmill is in many ways the heart of the town. The massive wooden waterwheel cranks all day and all night, and an eternal cloud of sawdust hovers in the air, scenting it with the aroma of industry and progress. Shouts of workers sound from dawn till dusk. A bustling business, the mill supplies a livelihood for many creatures . . . not just the expected beavers, muskrats, and woodchucks but also mice, rabbits, sparrows, and the odd mink. Even the rough-and-tumble river rats who navigate the lumber downstream are well aware of the sawmill's influence in the region. And over it all—quite literally, since his office is in the top of the mill's clock tower—Reginald von Beaverpelt keeps a keen eye on operations, making sure everything runs, in fact, like clockwork. Shady Hollow thrives with the mill . . . even if certain toads grouse about the noise and the sawdust.

There are other businesses, of course. The hardware store, the grocer, and the florist all flank Main Street's east side. The police station, the town hall, and the bank stand on the west. Turn the corner onto Walnut and you'll find Nevermore Books, a haven for bibliophiles of all stripes and spots. Fiction, mystery, history, poetry—everything has a shelf here. Other little businesses (the dressmaker, the haberdasher, the apothecary) nestle along the side streets Oak and Pine, and life is busy for the residents.

But Shady Hollow is not all work. Whether you first stroll down Main Street past River Drive or amble up Maple, Elm, Chestnut, or Beech, eventually you will find the true social heart of the town at Main and Walnut. Some grand establishment, you think? A church, perhaps? A great hall? A treehouse for the ages? No, and no, and no. It is a coffee shop, built low and unassuming under a grove of mighty sycamore trees. Inside, warm wooden booths have grown shiny with wear, and the rich smells of coffee and sweet fruit pies (the house specialty) permeate the very walls. This is Joe's Mug, run by a moose with quite a mug, as the always-humble Joe would not hesitate to tell you himself. Though he may not ever win a beauty contest, he's never lacked for attention, and everyone agrees that he sure knows his coffee. Most creatures start their days, or nights, at Joe's. And if there's news to be heard, Joe has heard it.

But don't think Shady Hollow lacks a more formal news organization. The august offices of the Shady Hollow *Herald* lie not one block away, just off Elm. You might pick up that morning's issue along with your coffee and peruse the latest headlines of this buzzing boreal hamlet.

For instance, today's headline story profiles the spelling bee winner, Ashley Chitters (mouse, eight years of age), and features a photo of the student proudly wearing a bright bee-shaped medal on a long ribbon around her neck. She has triumphed for the third year running, spelling *c-o-n-t-u-m-a-c-i-o-u-s* with no hesitation whatsoever to great applause. Her rival—a stoat who ironically was somewhat contumacious—tried to put an *i* in *lachrymose*, to his detriment. Next to the article on the spelling bee queen is a recipe for peach cobbler from the rabbits of Cold Clay Orchards. An accompanying illustration makes the mouth water.

Such is the news in Shady Hollow.

Other things happen, of course. There is love and hate, deceit and betrayal. There is loyalty and disappointment, heroism and villainy, all of a small order. But these things are, for the most part, private, and secret. They take place behind closed doors, or underground in dens, or among the branches that shade the town so well. You do not see them aired in the peaceful world of Shady Hollow.

But very soon, you will.

Chapter 1

One lovely dawn in late August, the sun was cresting the tops of the distant hills to pour its golden light over the forest. Gladys Honeysuckle, always an early riser, was already on the wing, more than halfway into her daily journey toward town. She was a hummingbird (as her name implied), and her bright green wings were always in motion, going about a hundred miles an hour. Her tongue seemed no different. Gladys had something of a reputation as the town gossip. Conveniently, she was well employed by the Shady Hollow *Herald*, the town's sole newspaper, where she wrote a regular column about town events and goings-on. Not a prestigious post, perhaps, but one suited to her gifts. BW Stone, the editor of the *Herald*, had kindly provided Gladys with a small desk in the newsroom, making her the first gossip columnist to rate as a regular reporter. This distinction made Gladys puff up her chest with pride and ensured her daily attendance at the paper. BW Stone liked all his reporters to be on-site, where he could keep his sharp skunk eyes on them.

Gladys was a widow, and her chicks were grown and gone. A true empty nester, she looked forward to going to work every day. Further, she was determined to prove her worth to the paper, thus assuring that her job would exist forever.

On this particular morning, she left her small straw-nest cottage, located high in a beech tree outside town, and flew toward the center of the village and the newspaper office. Peering down the quiet paths partly hidden beneath the leaves, she saw that almost no one else was about yet. She spied only Joe, ambling along the north track, his massive hooves surprisingly quiet on the road. The moose was not by nature an early riser—at least not compared to the birdfolk. But Joe wouldn't dream of allowing a customer to wait outside his coffee shop. He was up well before dawn to open the café, with fresh joe ready to serve. He seemed to be at work at all hours, with nary a complaint, despite being alone in the world but for his son, Joe Junior. Servers and cooks came and went . . . Joe was a constant.

Gladys paid Joe little mind while she winged her way over the forest. She had her own issues to worry about, *thankyouverymuch*. While she darted over the tallest branches, her buzzing brain was fully occupied with thoughts of her youngest, Heather, who had recently moved in with her new husband. They were both grown, true, but it's a mother's prerogative to worry about her offspring, and Gladys was no exception. Of course her chick claimed to be happy. They lived off in their own world, a day's flight away. But who really knew?

Not Gladys, who uncharacteristically was feeling quite left out of the loop and was rather anxious as a result. This was a state she *never* wanted to be in. She trembled at the very notion of unheard gossip.

Lost in thought, Gladys circled twice over the millpond, gaining height on an updraft. She glanced down at the water, yet to be touched by sunlight. Coasting on the wind, she spied something out of the ordinary, a shape that didn't quite fit. She swooped back around for another look. What could it be? A sack of some type? A bit of lost wood floating in the pond? She dipped even lower, her natural curiosity bubbling forth.

The object broke the smooth surface of the water, shapeless and perplexing in the pale dawn light. It was still and quiet, but it was no clump of weeds or loose log that had drifted to the middle of the pond at the behest of the gentle current.

The hummingbird's heart went cold. This shape was getting awfully . . . familiar. Her wings beating furiously, Gladys flew even lower, hovering directly above the body of a toad, belly up. And not just any toad. Otto Sumpf.

Otto was a longtime resident of the Shady Hollow pond. He had a reputation for being grumpy and surly, though some residents insisted that underneath the facade, he was quite kind. He would never thank you to point it out, though.

Now, it appeared, he was also quite dead. His pale legs were stiff; if not for the position of the body and its terrible stillness, he might have been midleap.

Stunned, Gladys registered these incidental facts while staring at the poor toad from a vantage point only birds enjoy.

From the shore, Gladys's actions would be unclear, should any-one be watching. She didn't consider that, however, because the horrible truth of Otto's demise was still coalescing in her frantic mind.

Dead! Poor Otto was dead! And she, Gladys Honeysuckle, was the first to know! At last Gladys glanced nervously around to see if anyone else was present. She had discovered a body, and she had to tell someone. Her tiny hummingbird heart thrummed with palpitations so rapid she thought she might faint. She had vital news of interest to the whole of Shady Hol-low. She *had* to tell someone. No, she had to tell *everyone*!

A small voice in her head reminded her that the police should be informed first and foremost. *That's right.* She nod-ded importantly to herself. The authorities had to be notified. She would call the police after she got to her office and calmed down a little. Though she was not terribly fond of Otto, he was—had been—a neighbor, and it was most off-putting to find one's neighbor dead on one's way to work.

Somehow, the shocked and sickened Gladys finished her flight, landing at the newspaper office. She hurried inside, hoping no one else had made it in just yet. But as soon as she entered the front door of the building, Gladys smelled the harsh notes of newsroom coffee. She knew exactly who it had to be—the fox.

Chapter 2

Vera Vixen was one of the *Herald*'s news reporters. She was also one of the few staff members who seemed to actually live in the newspaper office, and she had long followed the journalistic tradition of drinking her java strong, black, and scalding hot. It was brewed for effect, not for enjoyment. The quick red fox seemed to thrive on the stuff. Almost everyone else just got their coffee from Joe. To be sure, Vera often did as well, but her personality demanded a constant supply.

Vera was always hoping for a big scoop, and today was no exception. Her pointed ears twitched when she heard Gladys buzz in, and she braced herself for a chattering account of the latest gossip. Instead, Gladys hurried to her desk without saying a word, which was so unusual that the fox got up and trotted over to the little hummingbird.

"Good morning," Vera said with a smile.

Gladys nodded curtly and kept her eyes averted. Vera was not a top investigative reporter for nothing, and she noticed the smaller creature's gulping breaths.

"What's wrong, Gladys?" she asked. "You look upset. Did something happen?"

Gladys burst into tears. Concealing anything was against her nature. With only that small prompt, she completely forgot her resolve and spilled everything.

Listening to the hysterical hummingbird, Vera's ruddy ears perked up and her black nose twitched. A death? In Shady Hollow? Vera was naturally curious. This made her an excellent reporter. Though some townsfolk called her nosy, Vera paid them no mind. A good reporter, she believed, had to take an interest in things and ask the questions others were afraid to ask.

After wheedling the main facts out of Gladys, Vera settled the still-weeping hummingbird in her office with a glass of the bird's favorite sugar water and a stack of clean tissues. Vera's mind was working furiously. If Gladys had just discovered the body, maybe no one else had seen it. If she hurried, Vera could get to the scene and record all the details. The death of Otto would be big news, if only because everyone in town had been on the receiving end of the toad's rants at one time or another.

Unlike the hummingbird, Vera did not feel the slightest compunction about not going to the police immediately. The police chief of Shady Hollow was Theodore Meade, a slow-moving and slow-thinking black bear. He had no problem with things like shoplifting and noise ordinances, but that was about his limit. Vera would be happy to report the passing of Otto Sumpf to the authorities, but not before she had a look at the scene herself. She strapped her camera over her shoulder, ready to go.

On her way out, she peeked in at Gladys once more. The little bird was still gasping and wiping her eyes. As soon as Gladys regained her composure, she would be yammering to everyone who walked by. Vera had only a small window of time before the whole town showed up at the pond to view poor Otto's remains. She headed out of the *Herald* office toward the pond.

Fortunately, it was still very early, and few creatures were about, other than some folks headed for the sawmill, which loomed over the far side of the pond. Its mill wheel turned steadily, casting ever-widening ripples upon the otherwise glass-like water.

Vera strode on purposefully, her camera bouncing on its strap on her shoulder. She peered out over the edge of the pond. Purple loosestrife grew thickly on the edge of the water, with little green algae blooming just beyond. It was deceptively peaceful. Only Otto Sumpf was there. Floating in the water. Faceup. Just as Gladys had described.

Vera leaned forward and snapped a few quick pictures of the body. The ground near the edge of the water was soft and damp. Out of respect for Otto, she tried not to trample any of the paw prints. Even dead, Otto would likely not care for anyone mucking about his surroundings.

Out of habit, she took some pictures of the prints, although she was not sure if they would be identifiable. She paced around clumps of weeds, her nose twitching furiously. She noticed an empty bottle, too shiny to be trash, half hidden among the muddy stems of the pond grass. It looked like someone had flung the bottle toward the water, but the reeds had caught and held it aloft. She didn't touch it but snapped another picture.

Drawn to the specter of the dead toad, Vera glanced again at the body floating in the water. It was just a little too far from the shore for her to see much detail and certainly too far to fetch without a boat. She shivered at the thought of hauling poor Otto's body back to solid ground. She had never exchanged more than a few words with the beast, but she certainly couldn't imagine him dead. Was it a heart attack? Old age? Otto seemed like he'd live forever. Still, anyone can have an accident. He might have gotten drunk last night, misjudged the shoreline in the dark, and fallen in and drowned.

"But who ever heard of an amphibian drowning?" she muttered. "If Otto were to drown in anything, it'd be a bottle of spirits."

Vera was running out of time. The sun had cleared the tree-tops by now, and the sounds of daily life were beginning to stir all around her. She looked around just a little bit more before deciding the time had come to call in the police. Chief Meade could get his paws on a boat and get Otto to dry land, at least.

Before heading to the police station, Vera slipped into the offices of the Shady Hollow *Herald* and casually dropped her camera into her desk's biggest drawer, intending to pass by Gladys's desk to check on her.

Long before reaching the hummingbird's corner, she heard Gladys chattering and stopped short to listen.

"I got a shiver all up and down my spine, and then I saw poor old Otto just floating there . . . Oh, I knew when I woke up this morning that it would be a bad day!" Gladys yammered on to only the skies knew who. She seemed to have recovered fully from her ordeal. Vera noticed that she had had time to embellish her account, adding in the hints of doom that she hadn't bothered with when she first told the news to Vera.

The fox shook her head and turned tail, intent on reaching the police station before someone had a chance to waylay her.

The station was quiet, but the doors were wide open, so Vera entered without knocking. Unsurprisingly, Chief Meade wasn't in yet, but Vera reported what she had seen to his deputy, Orville Braun. Like his boss, Orville was a large bear, though of the brown variety and much sharper.

He told Vera he would go to the pond immediately to investigate and to retrieve the body for a proper burial. He knew the chief would not be in for a couple hours at best, even for something as momentous as a death. Orville, however, liked to get to the station and start his day in relative peace, long before his boss arrived. It allowed him to deal with the day-to-day issues of policing Shady Hollow. Working alone in the station also let him indulge in some grander dreams, in which Orville himself was the chief of police, adorned with a shiny new hat and badge and offered the respect and admiration of the entire town.

Perhaps his dedication would pay off now. He could take care of the sad matter of Otto Sumpf's death before lunch, and that vixen of a reporter would mention how competent and stoic he was throughout the ordeal. Yes, that sounded good indeed.

Coming back to reality, Orville warned Vera not to tell anyone else what she had discovered before he took care of things.

"Alas, that bird has flown. Gladys Honeysuckle was the one who told me," Vera said.

The bear rolled his eyes. "Oh, well. So much for keeping

mum." Deputy Orville collected his usual policing accessories—
a hat, rope cuffs, and a scowl—and headed over to the pond
with Vera at his side. She had not precisely asked to join him,
and Orville was still a bit sleepy. In any case, he didn't have
any reason to keep the fox away. He knew about Vera's reputation as a reporter. She would've been there soon enough
anyway.

"I'll have to commandeer a boat," Orville growled on the
way. "The chief took the police boat on a fishing expedition."

"What's he hoping to find?" she asked, curious.

"Fish, I'd guess." Orville looked blankly at the fox. "What
else?"

Vera stared back at the brown bear, suspicious. "A literal
fishing expedition?"

"Is there another kind?"

She narrowed her eyes, then sighed. "Never mind. I know
you don't see the inside of a courtroom that often in Shady
Hollow."

"Nope." Orville grinned, showing huge teeth. "Most creatures confess right away."

"I bet," Vera breathed. Orville could be very intimidating
when he wanted to be.

He was looking at the shore while they walked. "So I'll have
to find another boat now."

"The sawmill always has a few," Vera volunteered, "for
when lumber falls off a barge."

"Good enough," he grunted.

They reached the spot where Vera had taken her pictures
earlier. She said she would stand guard while Orville secured
a boat. She watched as the big bear hurried on to the sawmill,
his hulking form slowly shrinking in the distance.

She waited. After a quarter hour, she saw a boat making its slow way from the sawmill's dock to where Otto's body was floating. A few creatures had begun to notice that something was amiss and were now gathering on the shoreline to watch.

When Orville reached the body, Vera heard him give a startled yell, and she thought for a wild moment that perhaps Otto was still breathing. But the bear did not change his pace, suggesting there was no need for haste. He tethered Otto to the boat with a rope and then began to row for shore, toward where Vera stood.

A few lengths from land, Orville jumped out with a huge splash and hauled the boat up onto the mud. He saw the gathering crowd and roared, "Get back! Get back, all of you! Give us some space! Show some respect!"

Cowed by the spectacle of an enraged brown bear, everyone melted back . . . with the exception of Vera. She knew something was not right.

"Shall I help you pull him out?" she asked.

"No need." Orville waded over to the body and picked it up gently, as if it was a cub instead of a corpse. Showing no discomfort, he walked Otto's remains up onto shore and deposited it carefully on the cool muddy ground, facedown. The huge bear shivered once, not with disgust or even cold, but with anger.

Vera saw why when she got a better look.

In addition to the fact that Otto was facedown and unmoving, there was a dark trickle of blood seeping from his body, and most distressing of all was the hilt of a knife protruding from his back.

Vera stepped away, her insides lurching.

There was almost no crime in Shady Hollow, and to Vera's

knowledge, there had *never* been a murder. Otto may have been grumpy, but he was a resident and had lived near the mill-pond for many years.

"Who could have done this?" she whispered.

Orville stood at his full height, shaking off water. "I don't know, but I *will* find out."

If the deputy remembered that he worked under Chief Meade, he didn't seem to care. He could collect evidence, take pictures, and contact the Peaceful Hollow Funeral Home on Yew Street to collect Otto's body before the chief even rolled out of bed. Orville liked his job and knew he was good at it. It bothered him that he did most of the work while his boss took most of the credit, but it seemed petty to complain. After all, who really cared which bear solved the case of a stolen ice sculpture?

But now he felt differently. Petty crimes were part of life, but murder was an affront to civilized society. Otto might not have been the most charming neighbor, but no one deserved an end like this. Despite the situation, Orville felt some excitement in the pit of his stomach. Wasn't this the very reason he'd chosen his particular career? It was too late to protect Otto, but Orville could certainly seek justice for the murdered toad.

For her part, Vera also knew that this discovery would change everything. She left Orville to his work and fled back to the newspaper offices. For once, she had scooped Gladys on a story. Unfortunately, this was a tragedy.

But perhaps it could also be an opportunity.

Chapter 3

While citizens were gathering in horrified silence as Orville brought the body in from the pond and while Gladys was wearing out her little throat spreading her now out-of-date news, life was still blessedly normal at Joe's Mug.

Joe worked through his regular morning routine. He was enjoying his favorite part of the day—getting ready for the breakfast rush. He brewed the coffee, then packed the counter with various muffins and scones. They had been baked the previous evening and were now cool and fragrant. He filled the napkin dispensers (but not too full) and wiped down the tables until they squeaked. Joe took considerable pride in running a tight operation. He ran a dustrag over the counter whenever he had a moment and rearranged the muffins so that the fresh apple ones were in front. He wagered they would all be gone by lunchtime.

Joe heaved a sigh—and moose are capable of very great sighs, make no mistake. This was not exactly the way he'd seen his life panning out, running a café in a small village and raising his son alone. But the shop was what he had now, and most of the time he was grateful for it. Some days he never even thought about his wife, or wondered why she had left. Most of the time he was content if not happy, and he did the best a moose could do. He was well liked in Shady Hollow and thought to be quite a good creature, although he had never shown an interest in any of the single ladies he served coffee to.

A rapid knocking on the café door jolted him back to the present.

Joe started when he realized it was almost six o'clock in the morning. Time to open the café! He unlocked the door and turned over the Open sign.

"Come in, come in!" he bellowed to the squirrel who had been waiting. "One coffee, coming up!" Joe grinned wide. He was not going to dwell on his past today. That never ended well.

The squirrel was only the first of many customers. A mouse soon hurried in the door.

"Hullo, Joe! Just the usual!" said the mouse with a twitch of his whiskers.

This was one of Joe's regulars: Howard Chitters was chief accountant for Reginald von Beaverpelt, the owner of the sawmill. Howard was always in a hurry, as he was always running just a little bit late. He stopped in to pick up an assortment of pastries for the office every morning; it was common knowledge that Joe had the best in town, and only the best would do for Mr. von Beaverpelt.

Reginald von Beaverpelt was far too busy and important to pick up his own breakfast, of course. That was what he had Howard for. Even though the mouse was a clerk, he found himself ordered to complete all manner of odd jobs and less-than-glamorous commissions. Many creatures would not tolerate such treatment, but Howard's job was very important to him, as he had many little mouths to feed at home. He and his fine wife, Mrs. Amelia Chitters—the light of his humble life—had five small litters already, and he could tell you the exact number of children, too, if you gave him a moment to remember. Howard worked long hours and endured much abuse from von Beaverpelt for the sake of his family. Indeed, his and his wife's most recent litter of three meant Howard's job was more important than ever.

Fortunately, he was relatively well paid, and he was a very good accountant, always checking his work four times. He enjoyed his job. It also served to get him out of the house, which was often overrun with dirty diapers, souring cups of milk, and large piles of wooden toys lying on the rug. Howard adored his family and liked being a father, but he was also quite fond of his office at the sawmill, which had a door he could close. There, no one would disturb him except his boss, who could be heard bellowing his name from a good two miles away.

Howard checked his watch anxiously while Joe gathered his order. "Thanks, Joe! Please add it to the sawmill's account!"

Baked goods in hand, the tiny mouse bowed under the weight of his burden and staggered through the café door.

"Oh!" he squeaked, surprised by something outside. "Excuse me, I'm sure!"

"Hellooooooooo, Joe," a new voice called on the heels of the mouse's disappearance. Another regular patron of Joe's Mug in the early morning hours was Professor Ambrosius Heidegger. He was the one who had startled Howard—the unexpected presence of an owl will normally cause a mouse some discomfort, even in the civilized world of Shady Hollow. Heidegger observed a strictly vegetarian diet, though, having read much of its benefits. He taught evening philosophy classes to the older students in Shady Hollow and considered himself quite the scholar. He stopped into the coffee shop for a sweet sticky bun as part of his bedtime treat, since he still observed mostly nocturnal hours.

"Oh, and I'll have one of those fine seedcakes for this evening," he added today. "Much work lies ahead for me when I wake up!"

He needed sustenance to sit in his book-lined office, high in an elm tree outside town, and grade his students' first papers of the term. His work required a great deal of patience, as he considered most of his students morons. This may or may not have been the case, but at least they had the good fortune to learn from the great professor Heidegger! He thanked Joe for his service and left a generous tip in the jar by the register.

Joe kept busy throughout the early morning. There was a buzz in the air, not entirely due to the late-summer breeze and sunshine. Creatures chattered among themselves. Joe heard the name "Deputy Orville" and automatically listened more closely. Before he could make any sense out of what he had overheard, someone new interrupted.

"Good morning, Joe!" The brash voice belonged to Lenore

Lee. She was the raven who ran the highly popular Nevermore Books. Joe was not much of a reader, but Lenore was a regular customer and always quick on the uptake. She usually stopped in early for a coffee and a walnut scone and then headed to her store to do the accounts before she opened later in the morning.

Joe poured her coffee and put her usual scone in a bag. Lenore never varied her order, and it pleased her to see Joe have it ready just as he saw her coming.

"Lenore," Joe said in a low rumble. "Something's in the air." He normally didn't like to confess a lack of knowledge, but Lenore was a special case.

She nodded and lingered at the counter to add a dash of honey to her drink. "I saw a lot of commotion down by the pond. I think some beast might have drowned."

"Really? That's awful."

"Well, I'm not sure what happened," she admitted. Lenore was also loath to admit a gap in knowledge, but Joe was a special case. "I didn't want to gawk. I think I saw Vera in the crowd, and if she knows anything, she'll be sure to pass it along." Lenore and Vera were good friends, their comradeship stemming from similar inquisitive natures and a mutual love of the written word. "But I bet you'll know long before I do."

"I hope nothing bad happened," Joe said, already fearing it had. He felt a certain kind of worry in his bones. "I can't explain it, but I don't like it. Things are going to change around here."

The raven looked at him with her shining black eyes. "Change in Shady Hollow? It'll take something pretty drastic to do that." She gathered her breakfast. "One thing that won't change is me getting to work on time! Take care, Joe."

She crossed the street and opened the heavy dark oak door

of the shop at exactly the same moment as always. Lenore Lee was very particular, and she liked things a certain way. This was reflected in her successful bookshop, which was the only one in Shady Hollow (and indeed for miles around).

Traditionally, woodland creatures are not big readers, but things changed when Lenore opened the bookshop. *"Nevermore,"* she said during the ribbon-cutting ceremony, "will the town have to do without quality entertainment." Her vision proved to be a wise one.

Her cozy little store, repurposed from an old grain silo, was very inviting. Each floor was devoted to a genre of its own, with books lining the outer walls. The center of the shop was open, so that (with the exception of the ground floor) each level was really a balcony, where one could look down on incoming customers. The layout also had the practical feature of allowing Lenore to fly to any level in seconds. The corners held lamps and comfortable chairs where one could curl up with a mystery or the latest thriller. The store was also smartly located across the street from Joe's Mug, where patrons frequently took reading breaks to get a snack. Harmony among the businesses in the village was important. Lenore gazed over her small empire, but her thoughts lingered on Joe's news. She hoped Vera would come by soon.

Chapter 4

At that moment, Vera Vixen was in her office at the newspaper. She had acted quickly after leaving Orville. She bolted down to the darkroom below the main part of the building to develop the film in her camera. Now she hunched over her desk, studying the crisp black-and-white photos of the crime scene. Orville had looked like thunder when he brought Otto to shore, and she believed the bear would do his best to find the killer. However, she had more confidence in his intentions than in his actual competence.

In fact, Vera was fairly certain she was by far the most experienced investigator in Shady Hollow. She had worked the crime beat in a big city down south before opting for a quieter life in Shady Hollow. Not many of her neighbors knew about her past, and Vera wasn't inclined to enlighten everyone else. She had her own secrets, and she preferred to keep them close.

"Vera!" The yell came from the smoke-filled office at the head of the newsroom.

Vera sighed, rolling her eyes. She carefully tucked the pictures underneath yesterday's paper. Then she got up and hurried to the editor's office, where a shape slowly emerged from the cloud of smoke.

"Yes, BW?" she asked.

BW Stone, a portly but energetic skunk of elder years, glared at her from behind his massive oak desk.

"What's this about a murder?" He twirled his cigar as he spoke.

"I'm on it, BW," Vera assured him, coughing as the foul air invaded her lungs.

"I just heard about it from that sergeant—whatshisname, Orville? He wants to put a notice in the paper, and he won't pay for it!"

"He's a deputy, BW. And we don't charge the police to publish official notices," Vera explained patiently.

"Not charge? That's criminal!" BW snapped back, his cigar almost falling out of his mouth in his passion about fees. "Anyway, this is big. Huge. Momentous! You get on this story, Vera. I want a great headline and a full page of copy by sundown!"

"I have to find the facts before I can write them, BW."

"Then go, go, go! Everything in black and white!" he howled.

Vera hightailed it out of the smoky room, pausing at her desk only to grab the photographs. She would get everything in black and white, all right. Her nose twitched. She didn't need BW to tell her this story was big.

The fox reached the street in a few moments and looked up

and down before crossing. There was no danger in crossing a street in Shady Hollow, of course. Life moved at a leisurely pace here. But she sensed the mood in the air.

The everyday quiet of the town was shattered. Creatures stood in doorways, chattering to each other as the regular business of the day was forgotten. Since it was only cranky recluse Otto Sumpf who had been killed, the shock of the death could be handled quickly, leaving the inhabitants of Shady Hollow free to indulge in the delicious gossip brought by the murder.

She crossed to the shady side of Main Street and entered Joe's Mug an instant later. She looked around. Joe's was full of customers, all talking and worrying and speculating. It was like a particularly grim holiday.

"Vera." Joe had seen her and was already pouring her usual black coffee. "Here you go. It looks like you're on the story."

"So you heard?" It was a silly question. If there was news to be heard in town, Joe had heard it.

"Gladys stopped by for a restoring drink about a half hour ago. Her throat was rather dry this morning."

Despite the subject, Vera flashed a brief toothy grin at Joe. "Your poor ears."

"It's a terrible thing, Vera," Joe said seriously. "It's not right, what happened to Otto."

"Is murder ever right?" she asked rhetorically.

Joe paused, then said very slowly, "There might be a time it's justified." He seemed to be speaking to himself. Then he shook his head, the rack of his antlers scraping the ceiling. "But Otto never hurt a soul."

"He picked plenty of fights around town." Vera knew the toad's reputation as well as anyone, though she hadn't lived in Shady Hollow her whole life.

Joe was already shaking his head again. "All words! So he was a grump. Arguing with folks was his little game. He never did anyone harm by it. If anything, he hurt himself, living all alone down by the pond, his crankiness keeping other folks away."

Vera nodded, pulling out her notebook. "May I quote you?"

She asked Joe to share more about Sumpf, and the moose recalled some of the stories that surrounded the grumpy denizen of the pond. Sumpf, apparently, had come from somewhere in the farthest North, where the long nights of the frozen winters forced certain creatures deep underground for half the year. Joe suspected that survival trait accounted for Otto's habit of acting like a hermit, even in the relatively mild climate of the woods surrounding Shady Hollow.

The toad swilled down black coffee at every opportunity, which was why Joe had seen so much of him. But in more recent years, Sumpf had grown more taciturn and solitary. He'd rarely spoken to anyone in town on general topics. Even the genial Joe had barely got a grunt from him. Otto's longest conversations—if they could be called that—had been fierce arguments with anyone who got in his way.

According to Joe, only yesterday Sumpf had had a row with the great beast himself, Reginald von Beaverpelt, the unofficial mayor of the town. For the past several weeks, Sumpf had railed against the sawmill's dam for mucking up his end of the pond. After much goading, von Beaverpelt threw dignity to the wind and finally responded in kind, using some words too harsh for Vera to print in the paper.

"'Course," Joe said, "I'm not suggesting yesterday's argument had anything to do with Otto's death. He fought with everyone. He had words with Ruby yesterday, too. Set her up something awful. She looked a bit tossed coming in this morning. An hour later than usual and looking like she hadn't slept a wink."

In fact, Ruby Ewing had literally stumbled into Joe's Mug. Not one to ask questions, Joe greeted her and began preparing her an extra-strong beverage. Ruby, to put it plainly, was not sheepish when it came to her relationships. She liked a good time, although she was a good worker when she did work, as Joe knew well, since she had worked as a waitress at the café at one time. Ruby moved from job to job practically on a whim. Now she worked at Goody Crow's Restful Home for Aged Creatures.

With his usual tact, Joe had merely wished her a pleasant day and turned away to polish the counter to a sparkle yet again. Ruby had left as quickly as she'd come, barely speaking a word. Vera refrained from making a tart comment about how the sheep didn't seem to sleep a wink *most* nights. Joe, of course, was too polite to mention that part of Ruby's life.

Vera flipped her notebook closed. "Well, I'd best get moving." Knowing her next destination, Vera continued across the street.

"Lenore?" Vera called, peering around the bookshop. "Are you here?"

A whisper of wings was the only sound as Lenore floated down from the rafters. She kept her office at the top of the old silo, where no one could bother her.

"Hello," she replied, landing lightly next to the fox. "I'd say good morning, but it doesn't seem very good, does it?"

"So you know, too," Vera said.

"Everyone knows by now, I expect. News travels fast in these parts."

"I'm writing a story on Sumpf's death," Vera explained. "Did you know there's never been a murder in Shady Hollow before?"

"Well, not exactly." Lenore ruffled her feathers. "I was just rereading a few local histories. Shady Hollow was a bit of a rough town in its early years. There was a murder in my grandfather's day, when the sawmill was just being built. A worker was found dead at the site. They thought it was an accident at first, but it came out that he'd caught another worker stealing money from the construction fund. They discovered who it was without too much trouble, but he escaped before the police got to him. A weasel—I say without passing judgment," Lenore finished with a meaningful sweep of her wing.

"Fascinating! I can put that in my story," Vera said, scribbling furiously.

"I wouldn't have thought Otto had made anyone angry enough to stab him, though," Lenore went on thoughtfully. "I mean, he was a crank, but no more so yesterday than in the past decade."

"Someone must have felt differently," Vera said. "Or something else is going on."

Their discussion was interrupted by a commotion in the street. Alerted, the two creatures turned and peered out the open door.

Deputy Orville had not been idle. He was leading a raccoon down the middle of Main Street, paws tied behind the beast's back. The raccoon was loudly protesting this treatment, but the bear's grim expression showed that no argument was likely to change his mind.

Lenore cawed in surprise. "Orville's bringing Lefty down to the station!"

Vera jumped out of the bookshop and into the street. "Orville!" she called. "Are you arresting Lefty? Are you charging him with anything?"

Lefty took one look at her, recognized her from the *Herald*, and began to whine, "It's prejudice, pure and simple! Just because I been in a few bad spots, they think I'm a killer? I won't have it! I'll sue! I'll get justice!"

"Keep moving," the bear growled, "you show-off."

"Why are you arresting him?" Vera asked again.

"I'm not," Orville said sourly. "Just bringing him in for a few questions."

"But why? What have you learned?"

"Leave the investigation to the professionals, Miss Vixen," the bear said, his tone now lofty. "You go ahead and pen your little stories. I've got to find a killer. This creature's paw prints were at the scene!"

Vera stepped back, stung. She watched the bear hustle the raccoon down the street. Then her eyes narrowed. "My little stories, eh?" She flipped open her notebook. "That arrogant . . . I'll give Shady Hollow a story . . ."

Lenore took Vera in wing, brought her back inside, and spent a few minutes calming the fox. "He's all high-and-mighty, Vera, but he *is* a police bear. I'm sure he'll do his best to catch the killer."

"Will his best be enough? Orville's questioning Lefty just because he's the closest thing Shady Hollow has to a master criminal. Everyone knows it. But Lefty isn't a killer, even if his prints were . . . Lenore!"

"Excuse me?" the bird said, beady eyes wide.

"That's what I wanted to show you! I took some photos of the scene. Orville said Lefty's paw prints were there. Let's see what else was there. I bet Orville missed something."

"Easy bet," Lenore muttered. The two creatures gathered over the photographs, scanning them carefully. Vera had taken the shots well, and the images came through clearly.

Already familiar with the grisly images, Vera was pragmatic. "He couldn't have been stabbed in the water, of course; he would have been able to submerge and escape. So that means some beast overpowered him on the bank and then pushed him in . . . or let him stagger in. So do you see anywhere on the shore—"

"Here." Lenore touched a spot on one picture. "See the marks in the mud? Something wide, like Otto's body, was slid into the pond right here."

"That print *is* a raccoon's paw," Vera added, tapping another point on the same photo.

"But here's a beaver track. And a hoofprint. It doesn't prove anything, despite what Orville thinks. All creatures use that path. Except for me," Lenore added, lifting a wing, "and the other birds."

Vera was squinting at the picture. "There's more here than we can tell from these pictures. I think we should go look at the scene itself again."

"Won't Orville have roped it off?"

"So?" Vera tucked her notebook away. "Close up for a little bit. No beast will buy a mystery story until this one is solved anyway."

Lenore said, "Sad but true. Go on ahead. I'll meet you there."

Though it took her a moment to put up a sign and lock the

door, Lenore was soon airborne and passed the fox running along the ground.

When Vera arrived, Lenore was already there, peering at the scene. Orville had indeed roped off the crime scene, but the place had still attracted a number of spectators. Paw prints were everywhere; beasts had trampled over most of the ground, even within the rope barrier. Vera sighed when she saw the devastation. This was Orville's best work?

"There's the glass bottle that was in one of the photos." Lenore gestured with a wing to the bottle Vera had seen earlier.

"Yes, but it's been tossed into the reeds. It's too far out for me to get without swimming," Vera groused.

"Oh, never fear!" Lenore fluttered over to the bottle and snapped it up in her beak. Like any raven, she had an eye for shiny objects. She dropped it gently by the fox's paws, then fluttered to the ground. "What do you think it means?"

"Maybe nothing." Vera picked it up. It was a cordial bottle, dark green with a paper label depicting a flowering tree and some characters Vera couldn't read.

"It looks like the wine bottles at the Bamboo Patch," she said, referring to a new restaurant run by Shady Hollow's most recent resident, a giant panda named Sun Li. He served up tasty vegetarian cuisine, which was popular in the town. But Vera knew almost nothing about him. "I suppose it could be old. The restaurant did open several months ago."

"I doubt it." Lenore shook her head. "It's very clean. No mud, and the label hasn't come off from any rain yet. It can't have been here longer than a day or two."

"Do you think it's a clue?" Vera was gaining respect for Lenore's quick eyes and reasoned conclusions.

"Well, I don't think anyone stabbed Otto with a bottle. But

we could ask Sun Li if he sold one of those in the past few days, and to whom."

"Good idea." Vera put the bottle in her bag. "I can't see anything else at the moment. The ground is a mess! And until Orville releases Lefty, we won't know why he's being held."

The raven agreed. "We can learn more by talking to others. Let's go to the Bamboo Patch. It *is* just about lunchtime!"

Chapter 5

The Bamboo Patch was a restaurant in a low building on the east end of Maple Street. The roof curved up gently at the corners, and already the whole property was covered by a fast-growing grove of bamboo, grown from cuttings that Sun Li had brought with him. The tall grasses added an intriguing air; it looked like nothing else in the Hollow. The light green stalks sheltered the restaurant from the street, providing customers with a peaceful, secluded place to have lunch.

Raven and fox walked up a narrow, gently curving path of smooth white pebbles that led them to a bright red-painted door. Before either creature could knock, the door slowly swung open. A large black-and-white shape appeared from the darkened interior.

"Two for lunch?" Sun Li asked.

Vera had heard that the panda spoke more than a dozen languages and dialects. But then, she had heard many things about the creature, most of which she didn't believe.

Vera glanced at Lenore, who nodded. "Yes, please, if it's not too early."

"Right this way." Sun Li led them through the low-ceilinged place and over to a sunny spot by a window, through which they could see the lush bamboo growing outside. Their host poured hot tea into tiny delicate blue cups and then shuffled away to get menus. Lenore and Vera were not the first customers. Two young beaver maids sat in another corner—the von Beaverpelt heiresses, in fact. They were already nibbling on little stalks of vegetables.

Lenore picked up her cup and held it to the light, watching the sun illuminate the thin ceramic from the inside. "Pretty," she commented. The raven had an eye for such things.

"Do you like them? A few did break during my journey across the sea, but I was pleased that most of my dishes arrived safely," Sun Li said, returning with the menus, which were not much more than unrolled scrolls. "Special today is snap peas with forest mushrooms," he continued. "Very tasty."

Hearing that, Vera didn't bother to peruse the menu. "Sounds perfect. And what do you have to drink besides tea?" she asked, getting right to the point. Rooting in her bag for a moment, she pulled the bottle out and showed it to him. "Do you have something like this?"

Sun Li looked unperturbed as he took the bottle and examined it. "Of course. This plum wine is something I sell here."

"Can you remember who bought the last one you sold, and who kept the bottle?"

The panda considered. "Miss Ruby, I think. Earlier this week."

"Ruby Ewing?"

"Yes. She worked here right at the beginning, when I needed extra help to set up the restaurant. She developed a taste for plum wine. Why do you ask?"

Vera glanced at Lenore. The raven gave an encouraging nod. "We found the bottle near Otto Sumpf's body," Vera admitted. "But of course, it may not mean anything."

"It is often difficult to know what details make the pattern until one can step away from the whole thing," Sun Li said. He did not appear to have an opinion himself. "Excuse me while I prepare your order."

After he left, Lenore said, "Well, he doesn't seem terribly interested in Otto's death."

Vera looked out at the bamboo. "I'm not sure if he ever even met Otto. The toad wouldn't have eaten here, that's for sure."

"Not unless there was a special on flies and minnows," agreed the raven.

Lenore and Vera both fell silent as they mulled over Sun Li's connection, or lack of one, to the deceased. Shady Hollow was such a small place. It was hard to imagine that there were some residents who were unacquainted with one another.

It didn't take long for Sun Li to deliver two steaming plates to their table.

"I should have asked before," said Vera. "Did you ever meet Otto?"

"Well, yes," Sun Li replied. "He came here a few times after I first opened. He liked the lunch special, though I do wish he hadn't always felt the need to smuggle out his leftovers in a leaf wrapper. I have nice little boxes for that."

"He smuggled food out?" Lenore asked incredulously.

Their host nodded seriously. "He wanted to figure out how the sauce is made. Of course, that's a family secret." Without letting on whether or not he was joking, Sun Li gave a little bow and left.

The enticing smells from the plates drifted up, and Vera and Lenore tucked in, all thoughts of murder temporarily put on hold. Investigation was hungry work. However, the issue of the murder eventually resurfaced, and the two creatures began to talk about motives.

As Vera was considering whether it would be poor manners to lick the plate, she glanced over at the other occupied table in the restaurant and saw that the von Beaverpelt daughters were staring at them. They were a little too far away to hear what Lenore and she were discussing. But they were certainly interested. This instantly made Vera wonder why.

When Lenore, who was facing the other way, began speculating aloud about the likelihood of Lefty's guilt, Vera nudged her with a hind paw and gestured at the other table with her head. Lenore immediately understood and launched into a lengthy diatribe about the large number of bookstore patrons who often sat in her shop with a stack of books to look at but who never put any of them away.

"Do they really think I have nothing better to do?" Lenore asked in a querulous tone.

Vera nodded sympathetically and then glanced at the other table. The young beavers seemed to have lost interest in eavesdropping. They were gathering up their belongings, preparing to leave. They had quite a few belongings; it appeared their early lunch followed an extensive shopping trip.

Anastasia and Esmeralda von Beaverpelt were the only children of Reginald and Edith von Beaverpelt, and they felt their family name entitled them to the respect and admiration of the town in general. They were younger than Lenore, maybe just about Vera's age. Neither had worked a day in her life. Von Beaverpelt made plenty of money and lavished it upon his wife and daughters. They seemed to spend the majority of their time shopping, thinking about shopping, talking about shopping . . . and gossiping about whomever they knew. The von Beaverpelt girls had met nearly everyone in town, since their mother was on every committee and board.

It was widely speculated that Reginald von Beaverpelt had hoped his daughters would have married or left home by now, but neither option seemed imminent. Both creatures were attractive (in spite of very prominent front teeth). But Anastasia and Esmeralda were vain and silly creatures, which was the main impediment to future bliss.

They felt little but contempt for Vera, who was considered well turned out if a bit intense about her work. They had no use for Lenore either, not being readers or caring to shop at Nevermore Books. The sisters made a point of passing the pair as they were leaving the restaurant.

"Shouldn't you be at work, Vera?" asked Anastasia as she and her sister came up to the table. Esmeralda's many shopping bags almost swept the teapot off the tabletop; Vera made a grab for it, preventing an accident. She fixed the sisters with an icy stare.

"I am working," she replied quietly. "I'm pursuing a story on the Sumpf murder."

The von Beaverpelts exchanged a look. "And it led you to lunch, did it?"

"Where do you think it should have led me?"

"Oh, I don't know. I'm not a star reporter," Esmeralda snapped.

"Do you have any reactions to the murder? Did you know Otto well?" Vera asked in her calmest tone.

"'Know Otto well'? Who did? That old stump was always snapping at us, calling us useless warts on the ecosystem! I told him he knew from warts! Who cares about that old toad?" said Esmeralda, sneering.

They left in a huff. Lenore and Vera just looked at the sisters as they strode out the front door of the restaurant.

"Charming," Vera muttered as she watched them go, and then she resumed her lunch.

Lenore just shook her head. "'Useless warts on the ecosystem'! Otto did have a way with words."

"He had a gift for knowing what bothered folks, too," Vera mused. "Our heiresses do not like being considered useless."

"Maybe not, but they wouldn't kill Otto for saying so!"

The fox's nose twitched slightly. "Let's hope not. If we have to consider every beast insulted by Otto, the whole town will be suspect."

Lenore made a sympathetic sound. "We'll get to the bottom of it. And you have a story to write! Your deadline is only hours away."

Vera nodded. "It's got to be good. I may not be a star reporter yet, but I know everyone will read *this* edition!"

Chapter 6

In the afternoon, most residents of Shady Hollow were going about their usual activities, albeit with an unusual amount of nervousness. Deputy Orville, however, was not. His routine had been upended by the discovery of a dead body at the pond, and of course the chief was nowhere to be found.

Orville knew how to handle the first aspects of the case. He positively identified the corpse as Otto Sumpf, pond resident. He gathered evidence, including a sample of pond water. He also called the funeral home to come and collect the body following a medical examination. There would need to be an autopsy, but the medical examiner had to come from a neighboring village, as Shady Hollow did not have its own examiner. Orville sent a pigeon with an urgent wingmail message.

He was anxious for the official to arrive, since both jail cells were now filled: one with the still body of Otto Sumpf on the cot (not smelling yet but perilously close to that inevitable moment) and the other with the decidedly *not* still body of Lefty, whose talent for verbal abuse almost rivaled the victim's.

Ignoring Lefty, Orville stood quietly at the edge of Otto's cell, considering. He did not know the deceased very well, but still it was a sobering sight. Life was short and could be cut even shorter in an instant.

After a moment, the bear headed to his gigantic desk to prepare a report for his boss. The chief did not keep early hours (when he showed up at all) but depended on his subordinate officer to keep him informed about goings-on around town. Orville was almost looking forward to the chief's look of shock and surprise. Neither one of them had any experience in conducting a murder investigation, but Orville would put money on himself. He read quite a bit and had studied police procedure and investigative techniques on his own time. He was fairly certain the chief would have no idea what to do in this situation. But Orville was sure his boss would take credit for discovering the perpetrator, no matter who did the work.

The most important thing now was the *appearance* of progress. Thus, he'd sniffed out and arrested Lefty immediately. He'd needed to find the beast anyway; Lefty was wanted in connection to a series of missing jewelry reports in the Hollow's downriver neighborhood, which was Lefty's main hunting ground. Privately Orville doubted Lefty had anything to do with the murder. But he wanted to keep the town calm.

Not long after, the medical examiner arrived in Shady Hollow, slithering in all haste. His name was Solomon Broadhead, and he was an adder of considerable experience in all aspects of death. He did not inspire confidence in those he met (he tended to inspire fear and disgust), but he was excellent at his job. Most creatures he encountered quickly found reason to go elsewhere, but this did not bother Dr. Broadhead in the slightest. He wound his way up the suddenly empty Main Street and soon slid into the police station.

"Greetingsss, Officssser," he hissed. "Where isss the victim?"

Orville nodded to the cell where Otto lay. "Right there."

The snake slithered through the iron bars and into the cell, coiling around the body of the toad.

"Interesssting," he said, his tongue flicking in and out, smelling things no one else could dream of.

Orville turned away, shivering despite his heavy coat.

When the examination was complete, Dr. Broadhead came out of the cell to find Orville pacing back and forth in front of his desk.

"Yes?" the bear asked. "Did you find anything?"

Dr. Broadhead sighed. "Well," he began, "Mr. Sssumpf did not die from exsssanguination, meaning he did not die from the knife wound."

"Are you sure?" the bear asked. Otto had been stabbed in the back, after all. But he waited politely for the snake to continue.

"The caussse of death wasss poisssson!" Dr. Broadhead announced, and then he paused dramatically. "When I am csssertain about what kind of poisssson wasss usssed, I will let you know. I have sssome exsssstensssive tessstsss to run in my own lab."

"Thanksss, I mean, thank you!" Orville was somewhat taken aback at this news. After the medical examiner made his exit,

Orville continued to pace up and down the main room. This was a huge revelation. If Otto was poisoned, then he'd probably been dying—or was already dead!—when he was stabbed. Who would do that, and why?

Orville had hoped to impress his boss by wrapping this case up quickly. That was clearly not going to happen. Things were becoming more complicated by the minute. Orville stopped pacing, remembering Lefty was still cooling his heels. He had to question that lowlife.

The raccoon was stretched out on his bunk, staring up at the ceiling. He sat up when he heard Orville coming and started complaining again. "What's going on? Who was that creepy reptile? You can't keep me in here! I demand to see my lawyer!"

Orville was getting a headache and was in no mood for histrionics. He picked up a chair and placed it outside Lefty's cell.

"Shut up!" he growled. Surprisingly, Lefty did. "I want to know everything you know about Otto Sumpf."

"I don't know nothing, I swear," Lefty began to stammer nervously, seeing Orville's glare. "I may be a thief, but I never killed nobody. Why would I want to murder the toad . . . he's worse off than I am. Nothing to steal! You've got to believe me!"

This made sense to Orville, but still he was not ready to release the raccoon. "That's not much to go on. You can spend the night here," he said to Lefty. "We'll see if you remember anything else useful in the morning."

After making sure Lefty's cell was securely locked, Orville headed over to Joe's, where he ordered one daily special to be delivered to Lefty in his cell and another for himself to devour immediately. The deputy had had an extremely long day and was looking forward to going home for a few hours. The investigation would look better after he had something to eat and a good night's sleep. As he devoured his dinner (acorn mash with honey, and grilled apple slices on the side), he thought it would be nice if he had someone else to share ideas with. But then Orville realized he would rather work the case alone and not have to deal with the chief. Chief Meade wasn't all there even when he *was* there.

When Orville finally arrived home, he poured himself a small glass of fine woodland elderberry cordial. He was not a big drinker, but he did enjoy a libation or two after a long day. This day had been one of the longest he could remember, considering that Shady Hollow was not exactly a hotbed of criminal activity.

Orville settled into his easy chair to sip his drink and go over the events of the day. He had barely finished his glass when his head fell forward and he began to snore. This happened quite frequently, and Orville would startle awake in a few hours, hungry and grumpy. And though he did not know it yet, the next morning he was going to be very grumpy indeed.

For while Orville dozed in his chair, Vera was frantically working at the newspaper. Outside, the town was quieter than usual, and even the forest seemed devoid of evening birdsong and attendant twittering. Vera rushed to put together the story, squeaking in minutes before the deadline with BW breathing down her neck.

"Think of the sales!" BW said, his eyes uncharacteristically bright. "Everyone will want a copy. They'll *need* a copy. This is the story of the year! The decade! I hope the trial runs for weeks!"

Chapter 7

Vera barely made it to her den, where she collapsed on her soft bed. She was lost to the world until a bright ray of sunshine cut into her eyes.

"Too early," she muttered.

"Vera!" a voice called outside. "Vera, are you up?"

"Who wants to know?" the fox growled.

"It's Gladys. BW wants you back at the office right away! Orville read the article you wrote and went berserk!"

"He would." Vera groaned, but her ears twitched. Despite her tiredness, the fox smiled. So her little story got a rise out of the bear, did it? That was what she had been going for.

Gladys hovered by Vera as she emerged from her den and began to walk down Maple toward Main Street. The hummingbird chattered incessantly, and Vera nodded at the appropriate moments. Trying to get a word in would be pointless anyway.

Of course, Gladys had only one topic to discuss. News of Otto's murder had by now penetrated even the farthest reaches of the woods, in no small part due to the Shady Hollow *Herald*, which featured a full-page story of the crime (byline: *Vera Vixen, staff reporter*).

When Vera turned to open the door to Joe's Mug, Gladys burst out, "There's no time for coffee! BW said no pit stops."

"Joe's isn't a pit stop, Gladys. Joe's is a necessity." Vera swung the door open. Several pairs of eyes turned toward her as she walked to the counter. Copies of that morning's paper rustled.

"Good story, Vera," Joe said first, pouring her usual into a mug.

"Did you really find evidence the police missed?" a voice squeaked. It belonged to one of the older Chitters clan members, probably from the third litter. Vera could never keep their names straight.

Another creature said, "Orville was fit to be tied, I heard."

"Well, at least it made him read the paper," Joe noted dryly.

Vera nodded her thanks as Joe handed her the drink, and Gladys shooed off the few gathered folks to hurry Vera to the office.

It was bustling inside the newsroom, but the skunk sighted Vera immediately.

"What were you thinking, fox? Are you crazy?" BW yelled around his cigar. "Orville threatened to shut down the paper!"

"Whatever for?" Vera asked slyly.

BW picked up the paper and quoted:

> While having every confidence in the competence
> of the Shady Hollow constabulary, this reporter did

not find it amiss to examine the crime scene herself and discovered an object perhaps overlooked by
the police: an empty bottle of plum wine left at the
scene, possibly by the assailant. The proprietor of
the Bamboo Patch, Mr. Sun Li, identified the bottle
as one sold from his restaurant and recalled that a
similar bottle had been purchased only a few days
earlier. Why this avenue of inquiry was scorned by
the police is unknown.

This newspaper welcomes all additional evidence
that can be supplied. Any creature wishing to con-
vey information regarding the death of Otto Sumpf
may write to the *Herald*, care of Editor in Chief BW
Stone.

Anonymity will be respected.

"You all but called Orville a fool, Vera."

She flicked an impatient paw. "I report what I see, BW. You
told me to follow the story, so I did."

"There have been thirty letters to the editor just this morning!" BW yelled.

"Good or bad?"

"Are you kidding? It's great! Half of them think you're
right; half think you're wrong. A third think you're uppity, and
they're *all* reading—and buying—the paper!"

She rolled her eyes. "Well, I'm glad that's working out for
you. Now, if you'll excuse me . . ."

"Not so fast, Vixen. You have to go to the police station
right now and apologize to Orville. That's the only way to get
him off my back."

"Apologize? I didn't do anything wrong!"

"Do it, Vixen. Or you're off the story." With a final harrumph, BW spun around, indicating the conversation was over.

Without a choice in the matter, Vera headed directly to the police station. The stone building was shadowed by the large oaks growing along that block of Main Street. She found Orville behind a desk with the day's paper (rather crumpled and shredded) lying on top of it. Chief Meade was still nowhere to be seen. Lefty, however, was visible and audible in his detention cell a little farther down the hall.

Orville's eyes narrowed to slits when he saw her enter, and Vera suddenly questioned the wisdom of her bold article. A proverb about poking bears with sticks surfaced in her mind, but she couldn't quite remember how it went other than a general sense that it was a stupid thing to do.

The deputy was a very *large* creature, especially when he stood at full height—as he did now—and looked down at her less-impressive stature. Noticing the heavily muscled limbs of the bear, Vera fought an instinctive urge to flee.

"Morning, Orville," she said, trying to smile.

"Miss Vixen," he said in a low, worryingly calm voice. "Correct me if I'm wrong, but I allowed you to come to the crime scene with me. I allowed you to take pictures. I allowed you to see the body. And in exchange for such special treatment, you wrote *this*." One claw jabbed down at the paper on the desk, impaling the sheet.

Vera's hackles went up. "It's all true!"

Orville said, "It is disrespectful, and it makes my job harder. Don't try something like this again, fox, or I'll crush you."

She took a step back but refused to cower, despite her limbs' strong urging to do so. "Crush me? You'll have to catch me first, bear, and I can run circles around you!"

"We'll see, Vixen. At least you had a lot of fun writing your little news story."

"Not really. BW told me to poke around, and I did. I can't help that I found something you missed."

"You're just a reporter," Orville said with a huff. "Remember that I'm the only detective on this case! I am employed by the town to investigate crimes."

"And what about your boss?" Vera asked.

Orville snorted. "Do you see him here? Not even murder can get in the way of his fishing trips."

She saw an opening and took a different tack. She said, making her voice soft, "That must make it really hard for you, running this place all by yourself."

"No one understands how much work there is!" Orville groused. "Sure, Shady Hollow seems peaceful. But there's always something. Noise violations. Acorns through the school windows. Anastasia von Beaverpelt fell into a ravine last week while trying to take her own photo . . . And then there are the thefts!" He glared in Lefty's direction. "Twenty-five pounds of wildflower honey from the general store goes missing last week, and where do I find it? Under a tarp, in a rowboat on the millpond. Lefty hadn't got the time to row it downriver yet."

Vera fluttered her eyelashes. "My goodness. How'd you find it?"

Orville shrugged. "Tip from Sumpf, actually. Nothing much got past him. No wonder Lefty wanted revenge."

"I never poisoned him!" Lefty shouted from the cell.

"Shut yer trap, raccoon!" Orville growled, but the damage had been done.

"Wait," Vera said, stunned. "*Poison?* Who says so?"

The bear looked at her, then decided a little truth had to

get out. "That slithery medical examiner from the next county gave me details from his report. He said Otto drank poison somehow—or some beast made him take it. He was stabbed only *after* he was dead."

"So Otto drank poison. Oh, my . . . the wine bottle!" said Vera, realizing the true importance of her find.

Orville's eyes widened, too. "I'm going to need that evidence, fox."

"I have it here." Shaken by the revelation that poison was involved, Vera quickly fished the bottle out of her sack.

Orville took it, his massive paws cradling the glass bottle carefully. "Good. I'll send this to Dr. Broadhead to get examined right away. If this is what held the poison, I'll have a lead."

"So efficient. You should run for chief." Vera batted her eyelashes once more for good measure.

Orville drew himself up to full height again. "Wouldn't be half bad at it, I'd say." Then he lunged toward Vera. "And if you think I'd fall for flattery that transparent, you're underestimating me!" His bared teeth were about three inches from Vera's face.

Her legs shook, but she snapped back, "We'll see who's underestimating who, bear! I bet I can find the murderer before you do!"

She turned tail and vacated the police station.

Though he roared furiously, Orville didn't follow her. Vera counted herself lucky. There wasn't a single creature in the forest who wouldn't be alarmed at the idea of being chased by an angry bear.

As she trotted down the street, her mind was full of the new development. She realized not only had she provoked Orville further, she also hadn't gotten around to apologizing to him at all. Oops. BW would be climbing the walls if he knew how she had scrambled the exchange.

"After that, I'd better find Otto's killer first!" she muttered. "And poison! This changes things. Now to see where everyone really was the night he died."

Vera skipped past the newspaper office, not wanting to talk to BW and admit that she hadn't quite done what he'd asked. Instead, she went directly to Nevermore Books to discuss the nature of poison with Lenore.

As it turns out, Lenore had been brushing up on some elements of investigative procedure. She was nestled near the window of the shop, her beak in a book, in case any customers should wander in at this early hour. She had pulled several books on crime and murder and was plowing through them, taking careful notes. She was deep into one of the classics— a story collection about a beloved detective whose method of deduction was highly scientific. She hoped to find some guidelines for investigating a murder.

So far, she had written down a few key things:

- Capital mistake to theorize before one has data. Gather data, then see what theory fits.
- Eliminate impossible. Whatever is left (however improbable) MUST BE TRUTH.
- Reichenbach Falls = bad spot for getaway vacation

She had just laid aside her quill pen when Vera rushed in, her breathing still a bit quick from her encounter at the station.

"Lenore, I've just come from the police. Guess what? Otto was poisoned!"

The raven put down her book in surprise. "But you said yourself he was stabbed!" she said. "You saw the knife."

"Yes, but apparently that may have happened afterward. Orville said the medical examiner insisted Otto was poisoned." Vera shivered. "But he *was* found with a knife in his back. Who hated Otto enough to kill him *twice*?" It was horrible to think a creature in Shady Hollow could be so twisted.

"Or perhaps there are two murderers!" Lenore's clever brain started clicking immediately, devising possible scenarios. She had read about this sort of thing. The victim might have died following the first attack with poison. But if another creature came along and thought Otto was merely sleeping, a knife would finish the job. "That would mean two beasts sought to kill Otto on the same night. He was a crank, but surely that's beyond coincidence."

"Perhaps he saw something he shouldn't have," Vera suggested. Her mind went back to Orville's comment about Otto tipping him off regarding Lefty's honey heist. What if Lefty wanted revenge?

Vera listened to everything Lenore told her about murder investigations. She nodded as she looked over the raven's careful notes.

"So the first thing is to reconstruct where everyone was that night. We need alibis for every beast in Shady Hollow."

"Yes," said Lenore. "But remember, the alibis have to be confirmed to be worth anything."

Vera began by listing her own alibi. She had been home in her den, reading. "But I don't have a witness," she admitted.

"I wouldn't worry. I don't think you're a prime suspect." Lenore then told Vera that she had stayed late at the bookshop to deal with a new shipment and hadn't gone home until nearly midnight. She had seen Howard Chitters in the street on her way home. "He saw me, too, and waved, but we didn't talk. He often works odd hours for von Beaverpelt, and he must have been hurrying home to his family."

"All right. I'll go out and get more alibis. See you later!"

After leaving the bookshop, Vera stopped at Joe's once again, for both coffee and information. The coffee shop was relatively quiet for the moment. When Vera asked Joe where he was on the night of Otto's murder, just out of curiosity, he gave her a long look.

"Junior and I went home as soon as we closed the shop. We played cribbage for an hour, but we both turned in pretty quickly, what with opening the shop at dawn."

Vera believed him, of course. Joe had to be one of the most visible creatures in town. Skulking does not come naturally to a moose.

"I'm just trying to figure out who might have seen something. It seems we're a town of homebodies."

"I understand, Vera. Why not ask Heidegger if he noticed anything? He's a night owl."

"Good idea!" Vera perked up. "I can't believe I didn't think of that."

"Well, you'll have to wait until later, or he won't be awake."

"And I'll have to put up with his conversation." She grimaced, thinking of the pompous, long-winded bird.

"Good luck to you," Joe said as she ran out the door.

***

While the two creatures were discussing the new and confusing developments in the case, something else was happening at the other end of town. A creature ran furtively through the trees near the end of the millpond, on the opposite bank from where Otto's body had been discovered.

"Where is it? Where is it?" The creature was casting about, looking for something. "Should have done it myself . . . I knew I couldn't trust that beast."

At the sound of someone approaching, the creature fled before it could be spotted. It would not do to be seen here. Any suspicion at all would be disastrous.

Chapter 8

Although most residents of Shady Hollow were still speculating over Vera's incendiary article, a drama of another kind was taking place at the von Beaverpelt mansion. Reginald von Beaverpelt had been on his way out the door, his mind on several things he had to deal with at work, when he was ambushed by his wife.

"Reggie," she began, "I want to talk to you."

Reginald sighed; he had been so close to escaping without seeing his wife or his daughters. He loved his family, but a beast needed a little peace in the mornings, especially when he worked hard all day to make Shady Hollow the fine town it was. He tried to rush out the door and pretend he had not heard the dulcet tones of his spouse. He wasn't quick enough, though. In his haste to flee his own home, he dropped his brief-case, and Edith overtook him at the massive oak doors in the front hall. Reginald gave up.

"What is the matter, my precious?" Reginald asked sooth-ingly. Edith wanted to fight. He could tell. It was as clear as a storm cloud on the horizon. And it was about to rain on him. "Can we talk about it this evening?"

"No. This is *important*, Reggie." Edith von Beaverpelt did not have a great deal to occupy herself with throughout the day, so she spent much of her time needlessly worrying about things and fretting about her family, even though the von Beaverpelt daughters were quite self-sufficient. The only troubles they caused were the enormous bills that arrived from stores and creditors at the end of each month. Therefore, Edith focused her fearsome attention on her poor husband, who wanted only to go to work and to be left alone.

"I feel," Edith said querulously, "we are not spending enough quality time together and you are not paying attention to my needs."

To Reginald's ears, this statement sounded like it had come directly out of a magazine, which in fact it had. Edith read magazines religiously, though she was not fond of books at all (with the exception of cookbooks, which she regularly pur-chased for the help).

Not prepared for this, Reginald stared at his wife blankly. "Quality time?"

"And emotional engagement," Edith added.

He again tried to placate her. "Darling, I would be happy to discuss this with you later, but I have to get to the mill. Those things don't run themselves, you know." Usually this technique was quite effective, but not today.

"Oh, yes, always running off to work. You're always so eager to leave the house. What's on the agenda today?" she asked, her voice getting louder and more insistent. "Are you going to see *her*?" This last word was delivered at high volume, and then Edith burst into loud noisy tears.

"Who?" Reginald put on an innocent, confused face.

"That hussy," Edith spat, her eyes narrow.

"Brenda is a fine secretary and a fine young creature," he said quickly, "as you well know."

"That's not who I meant!"

Reginald had had enough. "I don't know what you are talking about," he shouted, though he knew perfectly well. "I have real business to attend to!"

With this pronouncement, he snatched up his briefcase from where it had fallen and stalked out of the house, slamming the door behind him. Edith rushed to the living room and collapsed onto the chesterfield, sobbing and touching a dainty, lacy pawkerchief to her eyes.

Both von Beaverpelt daughters had been crouching on the stairs, listening to their parents argue. Having little to no prospect of romance in their own lives—at least for the moment—they frequently eavesdropped on their parents. They read many of the same magazines as their mother, so they recognized the script from last month's "Can This Marriage Be Saved?" column. Esme was completely on her mother's side, being of similar temperament. Sometimes Stasia couldn't help sympathizing with her father, although she kept this little fact to herself. Her mother could be quite demanding, after all.

After Reginald stormed out of the house, the sisters waited a few minutes and then removed themselves from the stairs. Edith stopped sobbing not too long after the door closed behind her husband; she could have had a great career in the theater. As was usual after a marital spat, she would have the housekeeper make her a pot of tea to take upstairs. Edith would spend much of the morning in her bedroom recovering her nerves, as she put it.

The girls, though, had other plans entirely. Not even Esmeralda wanted to languish at her mother's bedside, offering sympathetic nods and picking up discarded tissues. They both wanted to get into town and hear all the gossip about the murder. They had each read Vera's newspaper article several times.

"Murder is so exciting!" Stasia whispered.

They dressed hurriedly and managed to avoid explaining themselves by shouting out a cheery farewell as they dashed by their mother's closed bedroom door. They were downstairs and out the door of the mansion before she could stop and interrogate them about their plans.

Their destination was Joe's Mug. The sisters never hung out there, preferring fancier establishments. But today they would make an exception since it was likely to be the center of all the town gossip and speculation.

Upon their arrival at Joe's, they stood awkwardly in the doorway, waiting to be seated by a hostess. Joe, who was extremely busy at the counter, spotted them after about a minute.

"Take a seat anywhere, ladies!" he bellowed. "If you don't want to wait for a server, just order at the counter!"

Anastasia and Esmeralda made their way to a tiny unoccupied table in the corner. They didn't realize it, but they were lucky to get the table at all. Joe's was hopping. Everyone in town had gathered to swill coffee and hear the latest about the murder.

The von Beaverpelt sisters settled in at their table and then looked wildly around for a server. Everyone else had food and drink, but how did they get it? Finally Stasia decided to brave the counter to get sustenance.

"You stay here and save the table," she told her sister. "I'll go and order our meal."

Stasia made her way up to the counter and ordered two large apple ciders and two blueberry muffins from the moose behind the counter. She was pleased to find that her order did not cost very much and that she had enough money in her pocket to cover it. (She was quite used to telling clerks to "add it to the account," but she suspected Joe's didn't have "accounts.") She waited as Joe made the drinks and put the muffins on a plate. Stasia returned to the table with food and drink in hand. At first Esmeralda sniffed suspiciously at her muffin, but after she tasted it, she scarfed it down with alacrity.

Stasia picked at her muffin more daintily while she looked around the coffee shop with interest. The von Beaverpelts generally kept to themselves since they were above it all. But Stasia gazed in wonder at the variety of creatures that made up Shady Hollow. And when she heard the word *murder*, she smiled. They were in the right place.

Chapter 9

Vera would have to wait until sundown to catch Heidegger and ask him anything, so she decided to track down others who might have been about on the fateful evening of Otto's death. Remembering what Lenore had said about seeing Howard Chitters, Vera began by heading to the sawmill.

The sawmill dominated the area outside town that was closest to the pond. It hummed with the sounds of chopping and sawing. The smell of wood shavings was everywhere. Logs were harvested upriver by crews of beavers and river rats, then shipped downstream by clever muskrat captains who could dance over the floating logs as easily as most folks walk on dry land. The river grew thick with lumber just upstream of the mill, slowing the water.

Part of the river was diverted into the millpond that Otto had called home, where the great wheel turned. It propelled everything in the mill and, by extension, the whole town. Dozens of creatures ran about on errands and special tasks, keeping the whole operation going.

After getting her bearings, Vera made her way to the central office, nimbly leaping over small piles of discarded wood and avoiding curious gazes (and occasional whistles) from the workers.

"Is Mr. von Beaverpelt in?" she asked the young beaver at the secretary's desk.

"Mr. von Beaverpelt is a very busy bea . . . creature," the secretary replied haughtily. "I'm afraid you'll need to make an appointment if you wish to speak to him."

"Well, I'm Vera Vixen with the Shady Hollow *Herald*. I'd like to ask some questions of the president."

"As I said, you'll have to make an appointment. He's not available at the moment."

"Oh, I see." Vera put on a disappointed expression. "That's too bad, since my article must run later today. I was hoping to get a quote from him regarding the possibility of the sawmill closing." Having delivered her barb, Vera smiled sweetly and waited.

The secretary gasped. "What's that? Closing? Why should the mill *close*?"

Vera knew she had the secretary's attention. "Well, should Deputy Orville be forced to drag the pond for evidence in the murder case of Mr. Sumpf, it will of course be necessary to shut down the factory for an indeterminate period. I expect von Beaverpelt is aware of the risk."

"Oh!" The secretary fluttered. "He never said—that is, we

can't close . . . Oh, dear. Let me just check . . ." She got up and hurried toward the inner sanctum of the president's office.

Vera felt quite pleased with herself for coming up with that little idea. Plainly, the notion of halting work even temporarily appalled the secretary. If work at the sawmill stopped, it would affect everyone in town. Vera knew she'd never get an interview with the boss unless he felt it was for his gain. He'd want to soothe his workers and his town so that no one lost confidence in the sawmill.

It did not take long for the secretary to return.

"Come this way, Miss Vixen," she said with a worried frown. Vera followed the little beaver down a hallway. It was beautiful, all done in richly paneled oak, with inlaid floors of pine and ash arranged in an alternating herringbone pattern. Vera idly wondered how long it had taken von Beaverpelt's workers to cut all those pieces, install them, and polish them just so the president could tromp on them every morning.

They reached the door at the end of the hall.

"Miss Vera Vixen to see you, sir," the secretary announced breathlessly.

"Come in, come in!" a bluff, jovial voice called.

Vera stepped into a room larger than her whole den. It was full of posh appointments and handsome furniture, but the focal point was a massive desk in the center of the room. Behind it, Reginald von Beaverpelt himself sat at ease, dressed dapperly. He was smoking a pipe and looked the very picture of an unconcerned executive. Only his eyes gave away that not all was well. They were tight and red, and they watched her quite warily.

"Always delighted to meet with a member of the fourth

estate!" he said. "Tell me, Miss Vixen, how can I assist you today? I have only a few moments before my next appointment."

Vera took out her notebook and pen. "Good morning, sir. I am reporting on the death of Otto Sumpf. I was curious to hear your reaction, seeing as it happened so close to your place of business."

"Well, I was saddened to hear of it, of course. We may not have been on the best terms, but a neighbor and all . . . Yes, very sad." Von Beaverpelt didn't look particularly put out.

"You had several arguments with him in the past," Vera noted mildly, writing in her notebook.

Von Beaverpelt put his pipe down with a bang. "Now, what does that mean? That cantankerous toad would argue with a tree stump! He said my mill disturbed his afternoon naps! I say his napping disturbed my profit!"

"I guess he won't threaten your profit anymore, sir."

Von Beaverpelt grew angrier. "What are you implying, Vixen?"

"Nothing at all. I'm just making an observation. Now tell me, what would you do if Deputy Orville instructed you to stop the waterwheel in order to drag the pond for evidence?"

"Stop the waterwheel?" von Beaverpelt asked, aghast. All thoughts of Otto flew out of his head. "He wouldn't dare! Besides, Chief Meade is in charge of the police in Shady Hollow."

"I think we both know how effective *he* will be in this investigation, sir."

"Meade's a very fine officer! Top shelf! Good bear!"

"You must think highly of him indeed, sir, considering how much you donated to his last campaign for chief of police."

"Now see here . . ." von Beaverpelt growled.

Vera hurried on. "Not that you have anything to fear from a thorough investigation. After all, you can't have been anywhere near the pond that night. Where were you, in fact?"

He snapped, "That's none of your business!"

"Was it somewhere interesting?"

"Of course not! I was at home with my wife," he ground out, stopping abruptly when he realized how his statement might sound.

Vera skipped to the next question before he could qualify the remark. "So you have no statement to make regarding the possible closing of the mill? No reassurance for the town?"

He stood up behind the desk. "Now see here. This mill is the lifeblood of Shady Hollow! Dozens of creatures and their families depend on its steady operation. Lumberjacks, carpenters, carvers, and builders. Even your newsroom uses paper made from my wood pulp. No one can afford to let this place shut down."

"Very good, sir." Vera dutifully scribbled down his quote. "Now if you'll excuse me, I must get back to make my deadline. And you have your next appointment, of course."

She backed out of the room before he could stop her and began to retrace her steps.

A small voice stopped her in her tracks. "Miss Vixen!"

She looked into the doorway on her left. The brown mouse Howard Chitters stood in the doorway of his cramped office. Vera stepped in at his impatient signal and noticed a door in a side wall. She figured it must connect to von Beaverpelt's office.

Chitters glanced at the door, too. "Miss Vixen, I couldn't help but overhear . . . Is it true that the mill may close?" His whiskers trembled.

Vera felt a stab of remorse. Her little ploy to get into von Beaverpelt's office had unintended consequences. Chitters, the accountant for the sawmill, had a large family and lived literally paw to mouth. He could not afford to have the mill close and miss out on a paycheck.

"It's not terribly likely," she hedged. "I wouldn't worry for your job."

"Oh, I hope not. This on top of everything else!" Chitters moaned. "It's almost more than I can cope with! With expenses so high now, we can't possibly lose any days of work."

"Is the mill in trouble?" Vera asked, her nose sniffing a new story.

Chitters wrung his little paws. "No! That is, not so long as we keep production up. But there's been a lot of spending. Too much . . ." The little mouse started to gnaw at a pencil. "I must—"

"Oh, there you are, Miss Vixen," a voice broke in. The secretary stood in the doorway, glaring at them both.

"Thanks for confirming von Beaverpelt's statement, Mr. Chitters," Vera said quickly.

"Goodbye, Miss Vixen." Howard turned hurriedly back to his desk.

"Let me show you to the door, Miss Vixen," the secretary said, her eyes narrow and cold. Vera followed her meekly, her mind in a whirl.

———

While Esme and Stasia were sipping their ciders and trying to listen in on the swirl of conversation going on around them, they noticed a figure making its way down Main Street. It was the panda, plainly dressed in his robe and heading south with a

distinct rolling gait. The other patrons of Joe's caught sight of
him ambling by. Conversations were hushed, one by one. As
he passed out of sight, talk resumed, but with a low muttering.

"Now that's a creature I'd watch out for," a chipmunk said
to his neighbor. "I've heard a lot of rumors about him."

"But he's nice, and we don't know any of that for sure.
Besides, that spicy cashew dish he makes is really good," the
chipmunk's partner said doubtfully. "You know, the one with
the little corncobs and the sauce that's so yummy . . ."

"Yeah, but what's *in* it? That's the question. I can never make
it at home! He's shifty, mark my words."

"He never talks to anyone . . ." another patron gossiped.
"And why did he move here, to Shady Hollow, all the way from
the east? He doesn't have family here, that's for certain."

"I heard he killed a creature in a fight in his home country
and had to flee."

This bit of gossip, though not new (and certainly not confirmed), was suddenly seen in a fresh light, and everyone who
heard it became briefly silent.

"Even if that's the case, I don't know why he'd have anything against Otto," said a more sensible creature.

"Otto made an enemy of everybody," said another. "And
who knows what sets off a panda?"

A squirrel said, "I heard he killed another panda with his
bare paws!"

"Well, aren't *all* his paws bear paws?" asked a ferret in a puzzled tone.

"I meant he didn't use a weapon!" the squirrel said. "Who
knows what else he could do? I think we were better off before
he showed up!"

There were angry mutterings of agreement, but not a few

tummies rumbled at the idea of never again experiencing the glory of a sticky rice cake with red bean paste, available only on Sundays. Could the panda really be a killer?

Esme gave Stasia a significant look. "Doesn't take much to get folks going, does it?"

Since the von Beaverpelt girls had never really known Otto or Sun Li, they could add nothing to the conversation. But they were pleased with the results of this little excursion. They had gained some interesting information. And Stasia decided she rather enjoyed the coffee shop's blueberry muffins.

Chapter 10

After Vera left his office, Reginald von Beaverpelt sighed and sat back in his desk chair. He didn't like the little fox nosing around his mill. He called his secretary and asked her to bring coffee. He had some thinking to do.

A few minutes later, there was a timid knock, and Brenda peeped around the door.

"Come in, come in," Reginald said impatiently.

She scurried in with a coffee tray, put it on his enormous desk, and scurried out again.

Reginald watched her go. She was young, about the same age as his daughters. He had wanted one or both of them to work at the mill office to learn the trade, but they refused. He had hoped for sons, strong young beavers who would carry on his legacy. All Stasia and Esme seemed to want to do was spend his fortune. The industrialist shook his head to clear it of this line of thought and poured himself a restorative cup of coffee from the ostentatious silver pot. He drank it black but for a teaspoon of sugar to make it palatable. Reginald took a small sip of the scalding coffee and settled back in his chair.

The conversation with the reporter had left him feeling ill. Closing the mill would be a disaster. Not only would it disrupt daily production, it might also expose some unfortunate decisions Reginald had made in a moment of weakness.

By the time he'd downed a second cup of coffee, Reginald was beginning to feel very ill indeed. What was the matter with him? This was not just anxiety. His vision began to cloud. His eyes fell upon the coffee. Had it tasted a bit . . . strange?

Panic began to well in the beaver's gut. Perhaps something *was* wrong. After all, there was a murderer on the loose in the Hollow! He began to cough but managed to call out to Brenda before sliding out of his chair and collapsing onto the floor.

Brenda came into the inner office, took one look at her boss lying on the carpet, and began to shriek. Soon other creatures, including Howard Chitters, streamed in. Someone—not Brenda—had the presence of mind to summon medical help.

Brenda was not all that fond of her boss, but this was by far the best job she had ever had, and she didn't want to lose it. If von Beaverpelt died, the mill would close, and Brenda would have to move back in with her mother.

Scant minutes later, Brenda heard a commotion in the outer office and two uniformed squirrels carrying a stretcher entered the room. They knelt next to Reginald's prone body and then rolled him onto the stretcher. One of the squirrels checked his pulse while the other asked Brenda what had happened.

In between sobs, she explained that the beaver had had a meeting with the fox from the newspaper and then had asked Brenda to bring him coffee. She had no idea what happened after that. "Is he going to be all right?" she asked the paramedics.

The grim-faced squirrels assured her they would do everything they could. Then they raced out of the sawmill office, carrying the unconscious beaver toward the hospital.

Since every beast in Shady Hollow automatically stopped and made way for medical squirrels, the pair carrying von Beaverpelt arrived at the hospital fairly quickly. The hospital was a small brick structure near the river, with large windows so that recovering patients could have a view of nature.

However, when the paramedics arrived at the hospital, they were surprised to learn that the town doctor was nowhere to be seen. After some frantic searching, they located a nurse who told them the doctor had been called away on an emergency. Two emergencies at the same time in Shady Hollow was unheard of. Months often passed without anything happening at all.

One of the attendants stayed with von Beaverpelt, who was breathing but still unconscious, and the other ran outside.

"Anyone know where the doctor went?" he chattered. "Or where the police are right now?"

A bystander pointed east. "Deputy Orville was just headed down to the Bamboo Patch!"

The medic nodded and twitched his tail as he bounded down the street toward the restaurant.

Fortunately, it was before lunch, and the restaurant was empty except for Sun Li. The panda stood calmly in front of Deputy Orville, who was holding an empty bottle. The paramedic was stammering the problem to Orville when, to the squirrel's surprise, Sun Li grabbed a small bag from behind a counter.

"I can help the patient," he said.

Sun Li flipped the restaurant's OPEN sign to CLOSED and led the way back to the hospital. The squirrel followed both bears in confusion. He didn't know what the panda could do, but he was relieved to have someone taking charge.

Upon entering the hospital and assessing the situation, Sun Li's entire demeanor changed. At once he became brisk and efficient, barking orders that the squirrels obeyed without question. They wheeled von Beaverpelt into an examination room, and Sun Li checked his vital signs. No one questioned why a chef was examining a medical patient. Sun Li announced von Beaverpelt had likely been poisoned and that they must dilute the poison with as much liquid as possible.

This procedure was carried out, and eventually the patient was out of danger. Von Beaverpelt was moved to a sunny room and told to rest. He babbled something about coffee and Edith, but the squirrels gently pushed him down on the cot and he collapsed in exhaustion.

Orville, who had gone to the Bamboo Patch to interrogate the panda about the bottle, now found himself rather flummoxed. If the panda was in any way involved in Otto's death, why would he save another creature's life?

"You look surprised," Sun Li said to Orville.

"I didn't know you were a doctor, Mr. Li. Um, that is, Dr. Li."

"It's actually Dr. Sun. With respect, there are very few things you know about me, Deputy." Sun Li paused. "If you wish to know anything else, you will find me at the restaurant. I'm happy to talk, but I do have a business to run."

Sun Li bowed silently to the two squirrels who had just watched him save the beaver's life, and then he left for the Bamboo Patch without another word.

The squirrels exchanged looks. They knew a real doctor when they saw one, and they couldn't wait to spread the news.

As Sun Li made his way back to his restaurant to prepare for the lunch rush, his thoughts were chaotic. His secret would undoubtedly come out. The news that he was not what he seemed would make its way around town in the blink of an eye. He once vowed he would never take lives in his paws again. But what was he to do?

Sun Li's real past had few details in common with the town gossip, but there were some glaring differences. Once upon a time in the country in which he was born, Sun Li had been a respected surgeon. During a routine operation on the prime minister's son, something had gone terribly wrong and the patient had died. Unfairly punished for this tragedy, Sun Li was stripped of his medical license. Not knowing what to do next, he had entered a monastery in the mountains.

After a few years of living and praying in silence, Sun Li decided that he had had enough. He left the land of his birth to seek a life in a country far away. Sun Li had always been fond of cooking, and here in Shady Hollow, his dishes were considered innovative and delicious. He knew the townsfolk were curious about him, but he never discussed his past. That part of his life was over. He was just a simple cook.

Until now. He headed into the Bamboo Patch and began to work in the kitchen, chopping vegetables with the assurance of a top chef . . . or a surgeon. Carrot slivers, peas, and sliced chestnuts piled up around him. Something was telling him that he would be unusually busy that day.

Chapter 11

Back at the sawmill, things were slowly returning to normal. Once her boss had been wheeled away to the hospital, Brenda had stopped crying and got back to work. First she sent word to the von Beaverpelt estate telling Edith that Reginald had collapsed and had been taken to the hospital. Then Brenda sent a message to the Shady Hollow police station, telling the officer on duty her boss had fallen ill under suspicious circumstances and they should send someone to investigate. The rest of the day was spent reassuring workers that nothing was really wrong and of course business would continue as usual. At closing time for the office (if not for the mill itself, which ran almost around the clock), Brenda picked up her purse and went home. She had had enough excitement for one day.

Shortly after Brenda left the office, Orville showed up to investigate the scene. Howard Chitters, still scribbling away at his little desk, squeaked in alarm but then let the police bear into the executive office.

After a quick look around, Orville took samples of the coffee and the sugar that remained on von Beaverpelt's desk. From what he'd seen earlier with Sun Li, this was another case of deliberate poisoning. What was going on in this town?

"Who makes von Beaverpelt's coffee?" he demanded.

"Brenda, his secretary, made it today," Chitters gasped.

"Where are the supplies kept?" the deputy asked.

"In the little kitchenette near the hall."

"And I suppose," Orville growled, "any beast can waltz in there."

"Well, yes, sir. Who would guard a kitchen?"

"Grand. Just grand," Orville muttered. He planned to make his way to the hospital to check on von Beaverpelt's condition. Orville sincerely hoped the beaver would pull through so the police force wouldn't have another murder on its paws. The two crimes must've been connected, Orville thought, but he didn't quite know how yet. He was really going to have to spend some time studying poisons. Perhaps Dr. Broadhead could give him some help.

Meanwhile, Vera paused at the office long enough to throw her next article together and get it to the copy editor in time for the evening deadline. The editor, a white rabbit of uncertain age—though he'd been working at the *Herald* since long before Vera started—took her handwritten pages and gave them a once-over, peering at the words over his half-moon glasses.

"Further developments . . . dragging the pond . . . possible halt to the sawmill . . . hmmmmm. What will the headline be?"

"I don't write the headlines. Whatever BW says, I guess."

The rabbit sighed. "Three guesses it will be doom and gloom so all the residents will wonder if they'll have jobs come winter."

"Well, BW knows his business." Vera shrugged. "I've got to catch Heidegger before he goes out this evening. Excuse me."

At the mention of Heidegger, the rabbit shivered involuntarily, though of course the owl had sworn off rodents long ago.

Vera made her way out of town to Heidegger's home, a truly vast and magnificent elm tree. He lived in an apartment about forty feet off the ground; ivory-tower jokes abounded whenever his name was mentioned.

Since ground dwellers could not knock on Heidegger's door, he'd devised a bell system. Vera saw a long vine snaking down the tree. Just above the ground, a small sign said PLEASE PULL FOR BELL. She did so. If a bell rang in Heidegger's quarters, it was out of her hearing. She waited as twilight gathered around her, casting the earth into shadow. The very tops of the trees still had a glimmer of sunlight on them, but darkness would come swiftly.

"Goooood evening," said a low voice quite near her.

Vera jumped. Heidegger had drifted down in soundless flight and now stood beside her.

"Good evening, Professor. I wondered if I might have a word with you."

"About the night of the murder," the owl deduced.

"Yes, in fact. I thought, because you are out and about at night, you might have seen something."

"I was out that evening, yes," he said, his huge yellow eyes unblinking. Vera understood why he made the smaller residents nervous. "I flew almost to Green Mountain and back, which should answer your unspoken question. My colleague Professor van Hoote will confirm I was miles away at the time Sumpf was killed."

"Oh." Vera was vaguely disappointed, though it was of course important to know Heidegger was not a suspect. "I hoped you might've been a witness to something important."

"Well, perhaps I can be of some assistance. You created quite a kerfuffle in town after beating the police at their own game."

"Finding the bottle of plum wine, you mean?"

The owl nodded. "I saw that same bottle in that very spot during the last light of day. At the time, it was only a flash of green. But after reading your article, I realized what I had seen."

"So some beast did put it there the day of the murder!"

"Perhaps just before I saw it, because a moment later I saw a creature hurrying away from the pond. Based on a simple calculation of trajectory and average speed, I am confident that the creature was walking from the location in question."

"Did you see who it was?" Vera asked.

"Alas, it was partially concealed by leaves. I could not get a clear glimpse from my heightened perspective. But it was a midsize creature. And it was moving quite furtively. You know, *furtive* comes from the Latin *furtivus*, or 'thief'; thus, *furtively* means 'in the manner of a thief.'"

Heidegger could never resist showing off his vast knowledge. He was without a doubt the most educated creature in

Shady Hollow, having attained numerous degrees from prestigious institutions the world over—as he never hesitated to point out.

A pompous old bird, Vera thought. But she could trust his eyesight.

"Have you told Officer Orville or Chief Meade about this?" she asked.

"They haven't deigned to interview me." Heidegger sniffed and twitched his wings. "Or perhaps they stopped by while I was asleep or out. Maybe Chief Meade found my tree to be too far from his favorite fishing spot on the river. It's where I've seen him spending most of his time."

The owl ruffled his feathers again. "That's all I can tell you, Miss Vixen. Now, if you'll excuse me . . ." He started an awkward run into the light breeze and was soon aloft, now graceful and deadly, soaring away into the darkening sky.

Vera looked after him, wondering how much the other residents of Shady Hollow had noticed without knowing the value of what they had seen. She decided that if the Hollow's chief could not be bothered to show up at his office, then she had no choice but to track him down at his home. There was no time to waste.

Chief Theodore "Teddy" Meade lived at the other end of town, near the river dock, in a den under a rocky hill that caused the river to bend in a long curve at the base of the rise. Vera saw a light on in a little window by the door. She knocked politely.

After a moment of studied silence, she knocked again, more aggressively. "Chief! Sir! Please open up!"

She heard a shuffling sound from inside. Then some steps.

Furtive steps, Vera thought.

The door opened slowly. "Oh, Miss Vixen," Meade said, trying to muster a smile and failing miserably. "How nice of you to stop by. Won't you come in?" Vera stepped inside the large home. A fish lay on the kitchen table, no doubt fresh from the river. The chief was in the middle of his dinner preparations. "How can I help you?"

"I'm following the story of Otto's murder for the paper. I was hoping you could tell me about any developments today."

"Oh, well. That is . . . yes. Of course there are developments. Certainly."

"What is the matter, Chief?" Vera asked, getting exasperated.

"Perhaps you should talk to Orville. Very capable junior officer."

"But surely you know what's going on. You are directing the investigation."

"I . . ." Meade looked panicked. "I don't know *how*! I've never had to investigate a murder before! Someone in this town is a killer! A maddened killer who stabs and poisons! Do you realize what this means?

"You didn't grow up here, fox," he went on. "No one in Shady Hollow locks their doors because we don't *have* locks on the doors. Except now the general store has ordered locks, which are coming in on the next barge. Ten families have already reserved theirs. What will we do?"

He sounds like Gladys, Vera thought. But she sympathized with the bear to a degree. He had been lulled into complacency by the years of quiet in Shady Hollow. Now that a crisis had arrived, he was utterly unprepared.

"What is Orville doing, then? He's never dealt with a murder, either," Vera pointed out.

"He's working from the *Big Book of Policing*. It has all the guidelines for what to do in any situation. We keep it on a shelf in the station. Actually, it was too big to fit on the shelf, so we ripped out the chapter 'Prisoner Beatings and Torture How-tos.' Who wants to know that stuff, anyway?" Meade looked miserably at the fish on the table. "Fishing is the only thing I'm really good at these days."

"So Orville is following a manual without the aid of his chief. Do you *want* the murderer to get away?"

"Of course not. We arrested Lefty!"

"On no evidence at all. Except that he's Lefty."

"Well, he might know something."

"You won't know what he knows until you know what to ask, Chief!" Vera shouted. "Heidegger told me he thinks he saw some beast leave the bottle of poisoned wine at the pond. Now you just have to track down and figure out who it was, and you'll find the murderer."

"We just ask everyone?" said Meade. "The guilty party will lie."

"That's why you get alibis," Vera said patiently. "Find out where everyone was that night. Get witnesses to confirm it. If someone is lying, their story won't add up. Then you have your murderer."

"You think it's that easy?" Meade looked hopeful for the first time.

"Not easy, but possible. Orville has started the work already. Now, will you go into the office tomorrow morning and help him?"

"Yes, of course." Meade drew himself up to his full height. "Shady Hollow won't be the same until this madness is over. First Otto is killed and then someone tries to poison von Beaverpelt. What will we do?"

"What do you mean, someone tried to poison von Beaverpelt?" Vera asked. "I just saw him today."

"Didn't you hear? Von Beaverpelt was found unconscious on the floor of his office. He was taken to the hospital, but the doctor wasn't there. You know who saved him? Sun Li! Who knew he had medical training? Lucky for von Beaverpelt, or else we'd be burying him along with Otto."

Vera was so stunned by this revelation that she couldn't speak. Was it possible that Shady Hollow was hosting a serial poisoner? She'd been researching the story, assuming Otto was the victim of someone who had a specific reason to kill him. But what if he was only the first of many? The idea was too horrible to think about. And Sun Li! She needed to find out more about the panda.

Chapter 12

Vera spent an uneasy night in her den, all too aware of her lockless situation. In the morning, she decided, it would be prudent to stop by the general store—just to look, of course.

The next morning, the woodchuck behind the counter said they usually didn't carry locks. "But you can add your name to the list of folks who want one. We've ordered a whole shipment from downriver."

Vera added her name, then thanked him and continued on her way. She was going to do something she should have done immediately: she headed directly for Otto's home at the edge of the pond. Otto had lived in a swampy area. A tiny secondary creek trickled slowly into the lower body of water, so the perimeter was soggy and overgrown with reeds. It was the perfect environment for a hermit-like toad.

It was less ideal for a fox, and Vera made a face as she walked through the muddy ground, her paws squelching in the thick goopy ground. She brushed past horsetail grasses twice her height. Then she found Otto's door; it was set into a low hummock rising slightly above the level of the bog.

Vera saw no sign of disturbance in the short time since Otto's death, and the only tracks were faint and cracked after a few days of late-summer sun. She gently pushed the door; it swung open, and the musty smell of wet earth seeped out. Otto had never needed a lock, either; his temper was sufficient in keeping creatures away. The structure was cold and clammy inside, its mud walls making a very effective barrier against summer heat and winter cold alike.

Vera stepped all the way in and looked around. She wasn't even sure what she was looking for.

Otto lived simply enough. If anyone needed proof of the toad's lonely existence, it would be obvious by looking at his living room. One chair was pulled up to a small table. A short stool by the fireplace could have served a guest if any came by. Jars of fruit preserves and dried bugs lined the cupboards. Otto had enjoyed a good raspberry-and-cricket sandwich, which was another reason he rarely entertained.

Vera noticed the cupboard held plenty of liquor, too. Bottles of wine, beer, and stronger spirits occupied the lower shelves. Her keen eye spied at least one distressingly familiar bottle . . . Sun Li's plum wine. Apparently Otto favored the beverage. She pulled the bottle from its shelf and put it in her pack. If it, too, was poisoned, the case would change considerably.

Moving beyond the sparsely furnished living room, Vera

found Otto's bedroom, which was even more humble. A low bed sat next to a small table, and a corner of the room had a curtain pulled across it, the space behind serving as Otto's closet. Vera pulled the curtain aside but saw nothing of interest. Only winter gear and a stack of pulp novels with yellowed pages.

She turned to the bedside table and finally found something promising: Otto had left a number of small black-bound books on the lower shelf. Another sat on top of the table. Vera picked it up and leafed through it. Otto had kept a journal!

Vera smiled as she began to read. Perhaps she'd find a clue. Otto was not one to write for posterity, though. His notes were minuscule in size, cramped, and often cryptic. He wrote in a mélange of languages, switching from one to another, sometimes within the same sentence.

His notes varied from the practical—*Remind Joe to fix alley door, swings open in wind*—to the vindictive—*VB looks furious on way to work. Wonder if EVB has been practicing her role in* Taming of the Shrew *again?*

Vera tried to read the last few days' worth of Otto's journal, but his style of writing was not easy to skim. She could not see anything immediately useful, but she decided to take it along to study. After a moment's deliberation, she took the other journals as well, figuring the older ones might be helpful if she had to write an article on Otto's earlier life. She felt a qualm as she put the journals in her bag. This wasn't exactly stealing, was it? After all, she was doing this to help find Otto's killer.

"I'll take good care of your journals, Otto, I promise," Vera said to the empty house.

She closed the outer door firmly and made her way out of the bog. When her paws hit drier land, she breathed a sigh of relief. Some creatures were simply not cut out for aquatic life. She scraped the mud off her paws and returned to town with a fresh sense of purpose. She would comb through Otto's journals. Surely something would leap out. Perhaps Lenore could help after she closed the bookshop for the day.

But first Vera had to go to work.

When she arrived at the offices of the Shady Hollow *Herald*, her hopes for a quiet session going over her notes were dashed. The office was full of noise. Creatures of all kinds ran back and forth. At least she was spared the steady beat of the presses, which usually ran at night. Vera spotted Gladys in the fray and trotted over to her.

"What's going on?" she asked, fearing the worst.

"BW is printing a special edition on the crime wave," Gladys replied.

"Two crimes isn't a wave."

"Well, I'm sure he's hoping a third awful thing will happen."

Vera sighed. She had hoped to do some more investigating before the entire town discovered what was going on. If only she could get BW to delay the special issue of the *Herald*. Although she knew it was highly unlikely, she had to try. She trotted over to the editor's office door and rapped sharply. When she heard the skunk grunt something, she decided to take it as an invitation to enter.

"What's going on, Vixen?" snapped her boss, an unlit cigar clamped in the corner of his mouth. "Haven't you solved the murder yet? The whole town is in peril. We need answers!"

"Sir," Vera began, "I really wish you would reconsider the special edition. I need some more time to interview the townsfolk about what they might have witnessed."

"Interview away! That's what I pay you for!"

"But by stirring everyone up about this, you'll only create a panic. Creatures will remember what they've read and talked about . . . not what they might have noticed a few days ago."

"Nonsense. The special edition will help them all think about it! I'm practically a philanthropist. I even had Amelia Chitters write up a recipe column: a soothing tea for jangled nerves. It calls for a full jigger of apple brandy."

"How truly thoughtful of you, sir," Vera drawled. "Look—when is the issue coming out?"

"Tomorrow morning, right before the toad's funeral. Special deadline is two hours later than normal. Get out there, type up everything you've got, and then let's sell some papers!" BW jumped up onto his desk in his excitement and then started bellowing orders to several rabbits with ink-stained paws who were preparing to set type. "If there's a mistake anywhere on the front page, you're all fired, understand?"

Vera took the opportunity to escape the office and get over to Main Street. She breathed deeply, trying to clear her head. She couldn't convince BW to hold back the paper. That meant she needed to find a break today, or it would be too late. The memories of any witnesses would be colored by the spectacular, breathless reporting of the *Herald* staff, all of whom were too beset with excitement and too intimidated by BW to write clearly. They'd put down whatever he told them. And BW wanted to sell papers, not find the killer.

So that left Vera. She didn't doubt Orville was trying his best; she just didn't think he was going about the investigation in the proper manner. Pouncing on Lefty was the easy way out.

Before Vera could decide what to do next, she saw Howard Chitters hurrying down the street. She chased after him. "Mr. Chitters! Mr. Chitters!"

He turned, alarmed. "Oh, it's you, Miss Vixen!"

"What happened yesterday after I left the sawmill? The chief said von Beaverpelt thought he'd been poisoned."

"He *was* poisoned. He'd had his coffee break, see."

"Poisoned coffee? From Joe's?" Vera asked, incredulous.

"Oh, no!" Chitters squeaked. "He has his own coffee service in the executive office. Brenda makes it. But she'd never do this. Someone must have snuck in and put poison in the coffeepot. Anyway, von Beaverpelt collapsed, and if Sun Li hadn't heard about the problem from the medical squirrels, the boss would have been a goner."

"Sun Li thought it was poison, too?"

"Yes. He knew right away. Brenda thought it was a heart attack . . . brought on by *your* questions, actually."

Vera snorted. "Not likely. I have to talk to Sun Li. Did von Beaverpelt stay home today?"

"Yes. I just checked on him," Howard confirmed. "He's issued the daily instructions from his bed. He's resting comfortably now. His wife and daughters are with him."

Vera wondered how comfortable anyone could be with the von Beaverpelt ladies hovering over them, but she kept her mouth shut. Instead, she directed her steps to Sun Li's restaurant.

The Bamboo Patch was quiet this early in the day. In fact, it would not officially open for hours, but Vera knocked only once before the door opened.

"How may I be of assistance?" Sun Li asked, bowing as he stepped aside and allowed Vera to walk in.

"I wanted to talk to you about von Beaverpelt," she said, getting straight to the point. "You saved his life yesterday. That's what I've been told."

"I did what I could. Fortunately it was enough."

"So you haven't always been a chef."

"Just as you have not always been a reporter," Sun Li returned. Vera stiffened as though anticipating some accusation, but Sun Li went on calmly. "We all have our histories. In my home country, I was a surgeon of some reputation. Then I left. I'm not a doctor now, but I am grateful my training allowed me to help someone."

"Yes, you prevented another murder."

"So it seems," Sun Li agreed, his expression troubled. "But it may not be enough in the coming days. You are a reporter, Miss Vixen. You look for—how do you say?—the 'scoop.'"

"Yes, I suppose."

"Then I will show you the scoop. Follow me."

Sun Li led Vera through the silent restaurant to the kitchen and then to a short hallway beyond, where the light was much dimmer. Vera stifled a nervous reaction. Surely Sun Li was on the side of good. He was a surgeon! Still, she should have told someone where she was going.

Before the fox's musings could get away from her, Sun Li stopped and opened a large cabinet on the wall. Vera peered in and saw a number of bottles and packages, many with unintelligible writing on them, though the contents of others were obvious. It was Sun Li's pantry.

"I keep most cooking items here, as well as some medicines," he said. He pulled out a small box from the very top shelf. It was loosely wrapped in paper. "This is heartstill—that is, it translates from the original language as 'heartstill.' It's a powder made from the roots of a very rare plant that grows only on mountain slopes where it mists but never rains. In extremely small doses, heartstill is a medicine, one used to soothe a patient to sleep or ease pain from an injury."

"What happens if you take too much?" Vera asked.

"You die," Sun Li said simply. "It is a substance that can stop the heart if used incorrectly. Hence the name."

"Do you think Otto and von Beaverpelt were poisoned with something like this?"

"I think they were poisoned with precisely this. I had two boxes of heartstill when I stocked this cabinet. I had no call to use the medicine. But after seeing the beaver's symptoms yesterday, I recognized the signs and took an inventory. One box is gone."

"Someone stole it?"

"I'm afraid so. Unfortunately, it could have been any time since I first opened the restaurant."

"Who else knows that this can be poisonous?"

"Everyone who worked in the kitchen and the dining room. I warned each employee not to use any item on this shelf. I explained that each of these products is dangerous."

"Who has worked for you since you opened?"

Sun Li gave Vera a list that included several Hollow creatures she knew. Most were those who'd worked odd jobs through-out town, like Ruby Ewing and the older Chitters children.

"I'll give these names to Orville. And to the chief," Vera added absently. "He'll want to know about this."

"The bears must look for the missing box," Sun Li pressed. "It contains enough powder to kill many creatures."

Chapter 13

W hat to do? Vera pondered her options. There were so many questions to ask and not enough time in which to ask them. Events were spiraling out of control like leaves in a windstorm. She had to put together a picture of what she knew. Only then could she see what still needed to be pursued.

She resolved to fuel her brain with a pick-me-up at Joe's Mug, but before she got there, she spied Ruby Ewing walking up the street from the opposite direction. She was dressed in a lovely outfit, one almost too fancy for a typical day.

"Ruby!" Vera called. "Do you have a minute?"

For a moment, Ruby continued on as if she hadn't heard. But as the two creatures drew abreast of each other, Ruby smiled warmly. "Why, hello. If it isn't the star reporter."

"Well, the reporter part is true enough. Actually, may I ask you a few questions?"

"Of course," Ruby said. "I was just going to stop for a drink."

"So was I," Vera said, herding Ruby into the building. Rather than step up to the counter, Vera pointed to a table by a window. "Let's sit for a few. Joe!" she called. "The usual for each of us."

As they waited for their drinks, Vera watched her companion and recalled what she had heard about the sheep. Like Vera, Ruby Ewing had not always resided in Shady Hollow. Once, she had lived with a large herd of other sheep much like herself, gamboling in a meadow and bleating contentedly . . . or whatever it is that sheep did when left to their own society.

However, Ruby was not like the other sheep. As Ruby grew up, her nature seemed to grow wilder. She craved affection and was seen with a new beau practically every week. She was egalitarian—species didn't matter to her. But every relationship ended in a row.

After a particularly public incident, she was ostracized by her family and cast out of the herd, left to make her own way in the world. She had come to Shady Hollow a number of years ago, and it seemed she had finally found a home in the small village.

Although Ruby had something of a reputation, she was indisputably a member of the community. She cropped weeds in the town square on her own time. She occasionally volunteered at the library. She'd worked at several places over the years and was currently employed at Goody Crow's Restful Home for Aged Creatures, where she seemed quite content. Those creatures who had problems with Ruby, those who snubbed her on the street . . . well, it said more about them than it did about her.

"You look nice today," Vera said, hoping to put the sheep at ease. "Are you going somewhere special?"

"No. Just work as usual. Why?"

"Your outfit is so pretty. Is that a ruby pendant you're wearing?"

The sheep touched the stone. "Why, yes, it is. Just a little joke, you know, because of my name. I got it as a gift because it's so me."

"Well, I can see why you'd want to wear it every day," said Vera, noting that Ruby didn't say who the gift was from. Maybe she'd gifted it to herself.

Ruby looked around the half-full coffee shop. "Are you still on the story of Otto's death?"

"Yes, and the attempted murder of von Beaverpelt."

"Oh, my!" Ruby jumped a little. "Of course it must all be part of the same madness. I can't believe there's a serial killer at work in town. That's awful to think about. I wish the whole thing would just go away."

"I'm sure we all do. But until the murderer is found, we can't go back to the way things used to be."

"You're very dedicated," Ruby noted. "More than the police, even."

"They're working at it, too, just in a different way."

The sheep bleated a laugh. "I've seen the chief work, darling. He couldn't detect his way out of a paper bag."

Then Joe arrived with their drinks. Ruby looked at hers—an extra-foamy latte with whipped cream and a raspberry on top—and sighed. "I haven't really been able to enjoy my drinks since poor Otto was found, you know."

"Did you know him well?"

"As well as anyone, I suppose. He wasn't as grouchy as he

seemed. He and I often chatted when I would walk past the pond. He had such an interesting life, you know, and he'd been so many places."

"When did you last see Otto?"

"The day he died. I had an errand round the pond. I waved to him as I walked back, but we were too far away to speak. It was maybe two hours before sunset."

"Had you been to the Bamboo Patch?"

"Why do you ask?" Ruby said, suddenly wary.

"Sun Li told me you used to work there and that you bought a bottle of plum wine from him."

"Oh, that. Yes, I do like plum wine. I developed a taste for it when I was a waitress there."

"Do you have the bottle you bought that day?"

"What? No, I don't think so . . . I lost it."

"You lost an entire bottle of wine?"

Vera's skepticism must have shone through because Ruby got defensive. "I put it down somewhere while running errands and forgot it."

"A similar bottle was found quite close to Otto's body."

Ruby looked very uncomfortable now. "Well, he had a sharp eye. If I left it round the pond, he must have found it."

"It contained traces of poison."

"Oh, dear!" Ruby gasped. "How can that be?"

"Perhaps Otto didn't find it first. Maybe the killer grabbed it and added the poison."

"And then handed it to Otto? That's vicious. Otto never deserved that. He was too good for that." Ruby stopped talking at this point and sipped meditatively at her fancy coffee.

Vera concluded that she wasn't going to get anything else

useful out of the sheep. She finished her own beverage and gathered her things together.

"Thanks for the talk, Ruby," she said to her companion. "I've got a lot of work to do. See you later!" With this, Vera returned her empty coffee mug to the counter and thanked Joe. She left Ruby sitting at the table, staring at her rapidly cooling coffee with its drooping crown of whipped cream.

⁓

While all this coffee consumption was going on, Howard Chitters hurried past the window of Joe's, ducking out of sight just as Vera emerged.

He was thinking uncharitable thoughts about Vera Vixen, the intrepid reporter.

"I certainly don't need that creature nosing about the sawmill," he said to himself in words he'd heard von Beaverpelt use. "We have enough problems without having our business printed on the front of that *Herald* rag." Howard was used to having his boss tell him what to do at work, and his wife did the same at home.

Howard Chitters had not always been such a timid mouse. Once upon a time, he had great dreams and aspirations. When he was younger, he lived in a large city. He had left his family's field to study accounting. This may sound dull to some, but Howard always enjoyed numbers, and he was good at making sure everything added up.

When he was living in the city, he met Amelia, a young attractive mouse trying to make it as an artist. They fell in love and got married. Their life together was everything Howard dreamed of—until Amelia got pregnant. Then it all changed.

Amelia abandoned her art and her loft and insisted they move to a small town where they could raise their first litter. The word *litter* struck fear into Howard's heart, but he reluctantly did as his beloved asked. They moved to a small cottage in Shady Hollow, and Howard took a job at the sawmill.

Amelia gave birth to five (yes, five) children. This was small as litters go, but it was big enough for Howard. Ever since, his life had been consumed with Shady Hollow, the accounts at the sawmill, the increasing number of Chitters offspring, and his wife. It may not have been everything he once dreamed, but it was all he had, and he wouldn't let that interfering fox take anything away.

Howard was quite relieved that Reginald von Beaverpelt would recover. Although he sometimes fantasized about being in charge of the mill, Howard had gotten far too used to doing as he was told. He hoped the boss would soon be back in his office. Howard knew that a few days of being ministered to by wife and daughters would be quite enough for von Beaverpelt. He would come sprinting back to the mill as soon as he could. If Howard could only keep that Vixen creature away until then!

Happily oblivious to Chitters's thoughts, Vera went back to the *Herald* offices and wrote up a few quick pieces. She detailed the situation of Sun Li saving Reginald von Beaverpelt's life, and she continued to piece together little facts about Otto. All the while, BW balefully stared at her through his office window. When she was finished, he bounded forward to grab the notes out of her paws before the ink was dry.

"Vixen's got her piece in! Set this type! The headline is 'Danger Stalks Shady Hollow!' Get to work, everyone. Everything in black and white!"

Time had flown by while she worked. Leaving the *Herald*, Vera headed back to her own den, taking the long way around, down River Street, which was closest to the broad banks of the flowing river. The town was quiet, and only a few creatures were about. She saw one squirrel in a fancy vest and coat walk by on the other side of the street—one of the bank tellers—but when Vera lifted a paw to wave, the squirrel only tipped his hat and rushed by. The mood of the town had certainly taken a dive. Vera sighed, then turned on Maple, toward her modest home. The stars were twinkling overhead, serene and unconcerned with all the chaos below.

Vera walked on, unaware she was being watched. A shadow followed her, lurking in the deeper shadows. When Vera got to her house, the shadow lingered for just a moment, then faded away.

Inside, Vera shivered without knowing why. Having no lock on her front door gave her pause, but then she shrugged. What could she do at this point? Take rooms at the bed-and-breakfast? To give in to panic would be letting the murderer win, and she had no reason to think she'd be the next victim—if there even *was* a next victim. The town's fear was making her silly, and it had been a very long day. Vera had planned to reread her notes and even begin writing another article, but the stress of running to and fro caught up with her. Soon after eating a few pawfuls of dried fruit (accompanied by a bit of carefully wrapped soft cheese to spread over the top), she curled up and went to sleep.

Chapter 14

The next morning dawned bright, but few folks in Shady Hollow felt very happy about the abundant sunshine and warm breeze. Most were scared. Parents counted their children. Husbands checked on their wives. And nearly everyone looked at their food just a bit askance, assessing even the most innocent of breakfasts for poison.

Vera woke early but did not check her food for poison—she was far too ravenous to think at all. After breakfast, she began to assemble her notes and made a list of those creatures she still needed to interview. In one way, her job would be easier today because everyone would be in the same place.

Today was Otto Sumpf's funeral. Woodland funerals were

not generally fancy affairs, but the hullabaloo surrounding Otto's death ensured this one would be well attended. Vera got ready well before time, dressing in a sober black that nicely contrasted her naturally red coat.

She trotted out the door, stopping by Nevermore Books to meet Lenore (already in black, of course). The two creatures headed for the cemetery, eventually passing through the gate, which was in fact nothing more elaborate than two yew trees growing in an arch across the path.

The cemetery was a quiet place. Huge cypress trees kept most of the grounds in shadow, so not much grass grew there. Modest gravestones tended to collect moss after only a few seasons, and the air was always cool, even in high summer.

A crowd had begun to gather near an open grave where the cloth-wrapped body of Otto rested at the bottom. Lenore looked all around, impressed.

"So many folks about, all chattering away and gossiping!" she said. "Otto would have hated it! The only thing keeping him here at all is the fact that he's dead."

"Hush, raven." Vera tried to suppress a snort. It was true; this was the kind of scene the toad had hated most in life. Solitary by nature, he had considered any group of more than one to be a crowd.

The townsfolk were arrayed in traditional black. Ruby Ewing was even wearing a chic little hat with a veil that covered the top half of her face. The von Beaverpelt ladies were all in attendance, though Reginald was abed, still too weak from his poisoning incident to be out in public. Edith made up for his absence by sniffling ostentatiously into a black lace cloth and commenting to all and sundry about "poor Otto" and how fortunate she was to have avoided losing her husband to the same fate.

"It must be a mad beast, to attack Mr. von Beaverpelt as well as poor Otto. After all, what did they have in common? Nothing!" she cried.

Vera overheard Edith's remark and exchanged a curious glance with Lenore. The beaver had a point. What *did* the two creatures have in common? Certainly nothing came to Vera's mind.

"The pond?" Lenore asked quietly so that only Vera could hear. "Otto lived there, and von Beaverpelt works there. Is a beast trying to drive everyone away from the pond for some reason?"

Vera considered it. She said, "The woodchuck family also lives near the pond, on the north end. We can ask them if they've seen anything suspicious."

"And warn them."

"Of course," the fox agreed. In her heart, though, she didn't think the pond had much to do with the poisonings. What could be gained by keeping creatures away? The pond had always been there! Besides, to really keep creatures away, the whole sawmill would have to be shut down. She'd suggested the very idea to von Beaverpelt herself, although she considered the possibility ludicrous. She'd only been trying to shock him into speaking. But now that Lenore had proposed control of the pond as a motive, Vera wondered if some beast *was* attempting to shut down the sawmill. It was awful to contemplate. The town depended on the sawmill; sabotage would be almost worse than murder.

At that moment, the parson cleared his throat and startled

Vera out of her musings. Parson James "Dusty" Conkers was a skinny jackrabbit. He was somewhat scruffy but very earnest and well meaning. He had served an apprenticeship in the vast western plains, working as a circuit-rider minister to groundhog communities in several counties. The long hours and sometimes dangerous conditions gave Parson Dusty a certain gravitas that most clergy took many years to earn.

Parson Dusty cleared his throat once more and then gestured for silence.

"Brothers and sisters of the Hollow," he began. "We are gathered here today to bid farewell to one of our own who was taken from us too soon. Though this toad may not have been the most charming creature to know, he was a longtime resident of Shady Hollow, and there's no one here who can say our village will be quite the same without Otto Sumpf."

"Yeah, it'll be a mite more peaceful now," muttered a voice in the crowd. It was immediately shushed by others.

Parson Dusty shot a look toward the disruption but went on. "Otto didn't make friends easily. He came from far across the sea, from a country where it snows nearly all year long. It's a hard place for any creature to thrive, and this toad left and crisscrossed the world before settling in Shady Hollow." Dusty's voice grew louder as he warmed to his subject. "Otto worked for years. As a sailor and a boatsman, as a stevedore, and even as a spy. Yes!" Parson Dusty nodded at the sudden murmur of the crowd. "He was deep in the Great Green Swamp during the Third Gator War! Not many of you knew that, I'll wager. He braved the dangers of the swamp's worst waterways to bring intelligence to the rebels. His work saved many lives, and it was there he learned the true value of silence.

"Otto never talked about himself much after that. He made his way north again after peace was attained, and finally he found a spot to call his own: the very millpond in the Hollow where he lived until his last days."

Dusty made a show of looking down at his notes. Then he gazed sadly around at the crowd. "Now, I said that Otto didn't make friends easily. Neither did he make enemies easily. He stood on his own opinions, and maybe didn't back down from an argument as often as he should, but he was ever so kind to the young ones in this town, and he never hurt a soul."

Several creatures murmured in agreement at those words.

"So we can't commit this poor creature to the ground without promising each other—all of us—to find the one responsible for Otto's death." Parson Dusty's voice rose again. "Now it's up to *us* to serve justice to his killer so that Otto may rest in peace, as he deserves! I call on all of you, brothers and sisters, to do everything you can to help the police find the murderer!"

The reaction was stronger this time. A few *amen*s mixed with clapping stirred the crowd. Dusty nodded earnestly, then put his paws up to silence everyone.

"There will be time to pursue the truth; now it's time to say goodbye to Otto Sumpf. Please, each of you take a little earth to cast over Otto, and remember him with kindness in your hearts." Dusty began by tossing a pawful of the soil that lay in a heap next to the grave.

"Farewell, Otto," he said. "I hope you find a swamp you love in the next life."

One by one, creatures began to follow the parson's example. Most only whispered a few words over the grave and quickly shuffled out of the cemetery, but several lingered for a moment, perhaps saying a more personal goodbye or considering their own mortality.

Joe even poured a bit of coffee into the grave. "This one's on the house, friend," the moose rumbled.

Vera saw Ruby sniffling heavily under her veil and noticed Orville cross his heart after making some unheard comment over the grave.

When Vera tossed in her own offering, she said nothing. But she made a silent promise to chase the story until she found the truth.

The wake was held—where else?—at Joe's. The creatures had been quiet at the funeral, but now they conversed as though they hadn't seen one another for a whole season. Parson Dusty's eulogy had been very effective if his goal had been to remind folks that Otto had been part of the town.

It also crystallized the feeling in the town that the crime was unconscionable, not to be tolerated. That the killer must be found and captured. That there must be a trial! Mr. Fallow, a black rat and a valued attorney with an office in the Mirror Lake neighborhood, was implored to take on the role of prosecutor once a trial began, to which he readily agreed. (Shady Hollow did not employ a full-time prosecutor.)

Orville used the time to corner creatures he'd been meaning to talk to, scaring them half to death as he demanded to know their whereabouts on the night in question. Vera, not above eavesdropping, dimly heard several variations of "Home! Home! Ask my wife and little ones!"

She duly appreciated Ruby's tart, gutsy rejoinder to Orville's questions, which came out along the lines of "You won't be surprised to hear I was entertaining a *friend* that night. You may understand why I *won't* divulge the name, Officer." Her suggestive tone reddened Orville's expression up to his ears, and he hurriedly sent her on her way.

"Anything interesting?" Lenore sidled up to Vera after about an hour had passed.

The fox shook her head. "Not really. It seems folks went out of their way not to leave their homes on the night Otto died."

"Convenient for the murderer," said Lenore.

"I just wish we could figure out *why* Otto was killed. And why von Beaverpelt was poisoned, too! Otto fought with him the day of his death, but even if Beaverpelt killed the toad in a fit of rage, he wouldn't pretend to be a victim, too, would he?"

"It doesn't seem like something he'd do," said Lenore. "And consider the manner of death." (Lenore had been reading a criminal psychology book the night before.)

"What do you mean?"

"If Otto had been killed in a fight or by a beast gone mad, he would have died from the knife wound. What I mean is, it would have been fast, and violent. But poison is methodical. You have to know in advance that you want to use it. You need to plan. You need to get the poison, and you need something to put it in. It's *not* something you use in the heat of passion."

Vera nodded. "I see your point. Could some creature have been trying to frame von Beaverpelt by stabbing Otto after the killing, to make it look like he'd been the victim of a fight?"

"But that doesn't explain how or why von Beaverpelt was poisoned."

"Ugh. You're right. This is so confusing. It's like trying to see through a fog."

"We just need to keep at it," Lenore said. "The killer made some mistake—in the stories, they always make a mistake.

We'll find out what it is and solve the crime. You'll be able to write the article Otto deserves, and the town can go back to normal."

"I hope so," Vera said miserably. "Right now I don't understand anything."

Chapter 15

Mindful of the panda's warning about the poison, Vera returned to the police station the morning after the funeral. Her last encounter with Orville had ended on a rather bad note, but she had important information to communicate to him now.

When she entered, Orville was sitting at his desk, studying some papers. As usual, the chief was nowhere to be seen.

"Hello," Vera said quietly. "Am I disturbing you?"

Orville glanced up, saw who it was, then straightened up in his seat. Vera saw his expression shift, but she couldn't tell if he was angry or merely annoyed. "Vixen. No, you're not disturbing me." Orville waved toward the papers. "These are the reports from Dr. Broadhead. He finally sent the results of his tests on the poison used to kill Otto Sumpf and to almost kill Reginald von Beaverpelt. Expert though he claims to be, he doesn't know what kind of poison was used."

"It's called heartstill, or it is in our language," Vera said.

The bear's eyes narrowed. "And how do you know that?"

"Sun Li told me." Vera related the details of her visit to the Bamboo Patch. She mentioned Sun Li's past life as a surgeon and then told Orville about the heartstill. Orville was scribbling furiously in his notebook, and he muttered that he'd get the rest of the mysterious poison that day and lock it up for safekeeping.

"Please understand," Vera told Orville gently, "whoever stole the first box of heartstill has more than enough poison to murder everyone in Shady Hollow. They won't need the second box."

Orville nodded but said he couldn't just leave it alone. "I'll take it just to be on the safe side," he said firmly.

Vera heard Lefty start singing in his cell. Orville turned around, too, saying, "I suppose I really should think about releasing Lefty. He's been enjoying a comfortable bunk and free food for far too long."

Vera nodded. She guessed that Orville knew Lefty was not guilty of these crimes, and Lefty didn't seem to have seen anything useful, either. The time had come to cut the raccoon loose.

"One less thing for me to worry about," said Orville, "although it has been nice to have some company at the police station."

He got up from his desk and headed over to the cell area to tell his prisoner the good news.

Lefty was lying on his bunk but looked up expectantly when

he heard the heavy tread of the police bear. Lefty scrambled to his feet when he heard the jingle of keys.

"Well, Lefty," said Orville, "I'm going to let you go. I know you didn't kill anyone."

At first the raccoon looked relieved, and then an expression of fear took over. "You can't do that," he almost shrieked at the bear. "I'm staying right here, where the killer can't get me."

Orville was clearly a little taken aback by the reaction (so was Vera, for that matter), but he put his key ring back on his belt.

"Okay, Lefty," he acquiesced. "You can stay in jail until we catch the killer." Orville walked back to his desk. He gave Vera a helpless shrug. "Never had someone beg to stay locked up before. Still, a few more days won't make any difference."

"Are you making progress on the case?" she asked hesitantly.

"Why? Have *you*?" he asked.

"Not really. I'm just reporting what I hear."

Orville glared at her for a second. "Ah, isn't it obvious? If I knew who the killer is, I wouldn't be sitting here."

"So what are you doing?"

"I've been asking questions. I just need to find out who put the poison in the drinks of both creatures." Sitting down at his desk, he pulled out a fresh sheet of paper and sharpened his pencil.

At the top, he wrote *Murder*. Then, on the left, he inscribed *Suspects* and proceeded to list the names of nearly all Shady Hollow residents, leaving off only children and police officers. He headed the next column with *Alibi for Otto* and then *Alibi for RVB*. "And that's just about as much as I've got. No one seems to know anything."

"Well, maybe I can help fill in a few of those spots," Vera

said. She shared what she'd learned of creatures' alibis so far, and Orville eagerly filled in the paper. He added what he knew as well. He even smiled once, when he crossed off a few names.

"I'm giving you the benefit of the doubt, Vixen. You say you were home alone. No one can prove what you were really up to . . . but if you killed Otto, you wouldn't be so persistent about the story."

"Well, I was home . . . alone. It's not as if I'm seeing anyone!" Vera blushed suddenly. What did it matter to *her* what the police bear knew of her personal life?

The door opened with a bang, distracting her.

"Chief Meade!" Orville said, surprised. "What are you doing here? I mean, good to see you, sir!"

The chief didn't answer immediately. He walked over to stand in front of his desk, which needed to be swept clean of the months of dust that had slowly been accumulating on it. Vera saw the chagrin on the chief's face.

"What news to report, Officer?" Meade asked in a loud voice.

"I know what poison killed Otto, sir. It is a rare drug that Mr. Sun has on the premises of his restaurant. He was once a doctor, and he says it is a medicine when used correctly. However, too large a dose—which apparently doesn't have to be that large at all—will stop a creature's heart. It's like falling asleep. Except you don't wake up again."

"Well, have you arrested the beast?"

"Who?" Orville asked blankly.

"The panda!"

"What for? *He* had no reason to kill Otto or to try to kill von Beaverpelt. He discovered the poison was missing a few days ago, but it could have been stolen months before that.

He never had a reason to check until now. We have the true weapon. Now we just have to find out who wielded it."

At that moment, Chief Meade appeared to notice Vera for the first time. "Are you talking to the press, Officer?" he barked at Orville.

"Um, no. That is . . ." Orville fumbled.

"In fact," Vera said, "the press was doing the talking. I merely passed along some information that the police surely would have got in due time anyway." She gave Orville a wink and was rewarded with a slight smile of thanks.

"That's right, Chief. Vera . . . Miss Vixen, that is . . . was most helpful."

"Well, that's how it should be!" the chief grumbled. "Let's remember who's in charge here after all."

"Yes, sir," Orville said, rolling his eyes.

Vera took that as her cue to exit. She said goodbye to Orville and headed back outside. Although Orville didn't know it, Vera had quite a similar sheet of alibis herself. She had managed to fill in several more spaces, though, and hers boasted an extra feature: Next to some alibis was a small red star. At the bottom, the star appeared again with the word *Confirmed*. Lenore had recommended the star method, and Vera was glad she did so. Thinking of that, Vera headed over to the bookshop to discuss the latest developments with her friend.

A short time later, the raven and the fox were hunched over a table in the bookshop, poring over Vera's notes and discussing the case from every angle they could see.

Lenore pointed to one name. "You can put a star next to von Beaverpelt for Otto's murder, I think. If he was an intended victim, it's not likely that he would be the killer for the first murder."

"But his alibi is weak," Vera said stubbornly. "He says he was at home, and Mrs. von Beaverpelt would never contradict him."

"Well, I don't have anyone to confirm my alibi, either," Lenore pointed out.

Vera shook her head. "I know you didn't kill Otto."

"And I know that you didn't, either. Or else your investigation is the best acting I've ever seen!" Lenore paused to take a sip of tea. "The fact remains that we don't have a lot to go on in terms of actual evidence. Murder's a funny thing. All the assumptions we make about our neighbors go out the window. Most of the time we don't care at all whether someone can account for their whereabouts at a certain hour. But then a murder happens, and suddenly the most respected members of society are no better off than the dregs."

Vera sighed. "That's a cynical take."

"I'm a raven." Lenore shrugged. "If you want sunshine and melodies, go find a swallow."

"I think the town's pulled together after Otto's death, just a little. We're all looking out for each other."

Lenore snorted. "That's because we're all looking out, period. The murderer has everyone peering over their shoulders. But when we look over and see our neighbors, we just have to say something neighborly. Do you have any idea how many times I was solicitously informed that the lock shipment was due Thursday at the general store? Anyone who doesn't buy a lock might as well sign a confession, according to the town gossips. Mark my words, if there's another murder before the end of this, we'll see what our neighbors are *really* like."

"I wish a few more of them were looking out before,"

grumbled Vera. "No one seems to have been around on the night of Otto's death. Heidegger admitted he flew out, but he was making a long trip. I messaged the colleague he went to visit, who confirmed that Heidegger arrived shortly after moonrise and stayed until well after the time Otto must have been killed."

"Heidegger was the one who saw a creature on the ground below, correct?" Lenore asked.

Vera nodded. "Yes. But he didn't get a clear look. The creature he noticed could have been anyone, based on the description. Well, not anyone. Not a mouse or a rabbit, for instance. It was bigger."

"What does that leave us?" Lenore began to list possibilities. "Beaver, raccoon, sheep . . ."

"Fox." Vera grinned.

"Fox," added Lenore. "Or badger, skunk, or woodchuck."

"But moose and bear are out."

"And finding the creature doesn't mean we've found a murderer."

"Maybe a witness, though," said Vera. "And we need another clue to go on."

"Let's back up," said Lenore. One of her books had relayed the maxim *Seek whom the crime benefits*. By tracing a motive for the killing, they could identify the killer. But there was such a dearth of evidence. *Why* was Otto killed? That's the question the raven kept asking herself. Try as they might, no one really knew why Otto was murdered. Without that crucial bit of knowledge, the mystery could not be solved.

"We must think about motive," Lenore pronounced. "Let's make a chart, like your suspect chart. Once we know possible reasons, we can eliminate the impossible."

Vera dutifully flipped to a new page in her notebook. "First possible motive: Otto was a crank who antagonized creatures as a hobby. Therefore, someone hated him."

"But everyone's had words with Otto at some point. That's an excuse, not a motive."

"He argued with von Beaverpelt regularly because the saw-mill bothered him with its noise and debris." Vera liked that possibility—it sounded plausible.

Lenore shook her head. "But again, von Beaverpelt never would have felt threatened by Otto. The town needs the mill too much to let a crank like Otto do anything to stop it running."

"And von Beaverpelt wouldn't have tried to murder himself, so it's unlikely he was behind Otto's murder, either." Vera sighed.

The creatures puzzled over other possible motives. Otto had been something of a busybody, so perhaps he had seen or heard some bit of gossip that proved more important than he knew. And though he argued plenty, he also loved to exchange news and tidbits with folks he ran into. By repeating what he'd learned to the wrong creature, did Otto make himself a target?

"Speaking of gossip," Lenore said, "we should ask Gladys if she's heard anything lately. Maybe she learned something juicy but held it back from her column to avoid attracting the murderer's attention, while Otto did."

"Gladys wouldn't have heard any gossip *from* Otto, though. They never spoke. Gladys always felt Otto tried to outdo her when it came to revealing bits of gossip."

"And she was the one to first see the body," Lenore said.

Vera caught the tone in Lenore's voice. "Do you think she knew where to look?"

"What better way to deflect attention than by being the one who reports the crime?"

The fox disagreed. "I saw Gladys that morning. She was beside herself. She's no actress! Remember her soliloquy in *A Midsummer Night's Dream* last year?"

With an amused caw, the raven nodded.

"I know she couldn't have faked the histrionics she was going through," said Vera.

"So it wasn't Gladys or von Beaverpelt." Lenore looked through Vera's notes for the fox's *Herald* articles. "It says here that Joe told you Ruby stumbled through town early that day."

"Yes, but Ruby had no reason to kill Otto. If anything, she was nicer to him than most. She was upset by his death. I could tell when I interviewed her."

"He was poisoned with her wine."

"Perhaps she felt guilty, since the murderer took advantage of her carelessness."

Lenore sighed. "All this gets us nowhere. We can't complete this puzzle without another piece."

"With our luck, the next piece will be another body," Vera said. Then she made the well-known forest sign of the jinx to prevent her hasty words from coming true.

Chapter 16

Vera still had plenty of work ahead. "I have to stop by the newspaper," she said, yawning. "Maybe we got an anonymous tip!"

But on the way to the newsroom, Vera had to admit she was up to her attractively pointed ears in suspects and alibis. She didn't feel she was getting any closer to discovering the identity of the murderer stalking the townsfolk of Shady Hollow.

She looked longingly into the windows of Joe's on the way but skipped the indulgence. She had been spending way too much time at Joe's, and the habit was not being kind to her wallet or her nerves. While the café was far and away the best place in town to listen to gossip, she hadn't heard any useful tips for a while.

When the reporter reached her office, she saw a single pink message slip lying in the center of her desk. It read: *Von Beaverpelt wants a meeting. He's at home.* There was nothing else on the slip. Vera knew better than to question the support staff at the newspaper. No one would admit to having taken the message. The rabbits were so frantic trying to get out the special edition for BW, she was lucky they passed on messages at all. She assumed Reginald von Beaverpelt had something to tell her, and she felt a little thrill of excitement in her stomach. Could this be the break she was looking for? Did the beaver know something about the identity of the killer?

But when Vera arrived at the von Beaverpelt mansion, security was tight. Anastasia, the elder daughter, answered the door to Vera's firm knock.

"What do you want, fox?" she asked rudely, standing in the doorway and blocking Vera's way.

She began, "I'm here to see your father—"

Before she could finish, Stasia cut in, "Papa can't see anyone. He is quite ill, you know."

Vera was not a star reporter for nothing. She placed her hind paw over the threshold and pushed her way past the young beaver.

"You don't understand," she said, heading briskly for the stairs. "Your father *asked* to see me, and you are not going to stand in my way."

With those words, Vera trotted swiftly up the curving staircase and raced down an unfamiliar hallway in search of the master bedroom. She could hear Anastasia shouting behind her, alerting the rest of the house to the intruder in their midst.

The hallway was richly carpeted, and family portraits in fancy gold frames lined the walls. However, since she had to beat the family to Reginald's room, Vera barely glanced at them as she made her way to a closed door at the end of the corridor. She knocked lightly and tried the doorknob.

"Hello?" she called. "Anyone in there?"

"Come in," said a voice. It sounded quite a bit weaker than the one she was used to hearing from Reginald von Beaverpelt.

Vera pushed open the door and entered the room. The beaver was lying on a mahogany four-poster bed with numerous pillows and a fluffy down comforter. When he saw his visitor, he sat up straighter in the bed and smoothed down his wrinkled pajamas.

"Miss Vixen," he began, clearing his throat, "I see you got my message."

Before Vera moved away from the door, she reached to turn the lock from the inside. That should keep the missus and her daughters away until Vera got her story. Then she moved over to the bed where von Beaverpelt lay and asked him how he was feeling.

"How would you feel," he answered, "if someone tried to *kill* you?"

Vera decided to skip the pleasantries and pulled out her notebook.

"What can you tell me about the incident? Do you know who poisoned you?" she asked, getting right to the point. "Who in this town would have reason to try that?"

"Know who it was? You bet I do!" the beaver answered, much quicker than she had expected.

"Well?" she prompted.

Reginald looked at her craftily. "I can't just spit it out. What if the killer gets word before the police can take action?"

Vera put the notebook down. "Do you want me to get the

police for you? You can tell Deputy Orville directly. He's quite capable."

"No, I can't," Reginald said quickly. "In fact, I'd rather not involve the police at all!"

"You don't think it's too late for that?"

The beaver coughed. "It's just . . . the police will have questions, you see. And it's better if . . . Not all questions need answers!" he concluded suddenly.

"I can't really agree with you there," Vera said. "Finding answers is my job, you see. But let's cut to the chase: What *do* you want me to do?"

Reginald looked miserable. "It's a delicate situation, Miss Vixen. If I promise you an exclusive . . . with a bonus, perhaps . . . would you report the story I tell you?"

"Go on," Vera said, her eyes narrowing.

"You see, I'm really afraid that—"

At this all-too-interesting moment, there came a banging and a shrieking from the other side of the door. All three ladies in the von Beaverpelt family were pounding on the heavy oak.

"What's going on in there? Why is this locked?" came Edith's voice.

"Don't talk to that vixen!" and "Papa is too weak!" were shouted simultaneously—the daughters.

Reginald looked at the door and then back at Vera helplessly.

A spare key rattled in the lock and the door burst open. Edith, Anastasia, and Esmeralda came pouring into the room. They glared at Vera accusingly.

"We'll talk later," Reginald whispered to her and lay back weakly on the bed.

Vera took this opportunity to gather up her things and head

for freedom. She brushed past the outraged beavers and trotted down the hall and the winding staircase. She swept out the front door, her mind in a whirl. She had been so close to getting something important out of von Beaverpelt! Who knew when she would have another opportunity to talk to him?

Chapter 17

Vera stomped back to the Shady Hollow Herald offices, frustrated and annoyed. *Von Beaverpelt is afraid of his wife and daughters,* she thought. Vera had to find a way to interview him alone. He knew something—that much was obvious. And what had he meant by *a bonus*? Was he suggesting a bribe?

When Vera reached her office, she saw that once again there was a pink message slip placed carefully in the middle of her desk. This one said, *Come ALONE to the large stand of oak trees in the woods north of town at midnight if you want a scoop.* Again, there was no mention of the sender or who took the message. Vera was intrigued but also nervous. It might be dangerous, but her curiosity would not let her stay home.

She decided to stop by the bookstore again and tell Lenore about the secret meeting in the woods. That way, if anything happened to her, at least one other creature would know her whereabouts. Vera entered Nevermore Books to find the raven dusting shelves and straightening the books. After hearing of Vera's plans, Lenore was quite disapproving.

"That's so dangerous," she warned. "Anything could happen to you all alone in the woods. Why don't you at least tell Orville?"

Vera shook her head. "No. Whoever sent this note would never tell a cop what they know! I have to go alone, or I'll never find out anything."

"You can't go alone," Lenore insisted. "I'll fly along. I won't let anyone see me, but I'll go to the edge of the river, just beyond the oaks. If you don't meet me there a few minutes after midnight, I'll come find you."

"I don't like the idea of putting you in danger."

"*Pssh*," the raven scoffed. "When you're leaping headfirst into danger? You can't have all the fun on this little adventure."

The hours till midnight were anything but slow. Vera sat in Lenore's bookshop and feverishly worked, hastily penning her headline article on the developments of the case for the paper. She had no respect for creatures who fancied themselves reporters but couldn't be bothered to actually meet deadlines. She'd known such a beast in her previous life in the big city: a rat who'd considered himself the Greatest Investigative Reporter of All Time. Vera once predicted the world would literally have to end before he actually filed a report, and she'd never seen evidence to the contrary. Vera, on the other hand, was diligent.

Her article mentioned the facts that the chief was now personally involved in the investigation and the discovery of the actual poison as revealed by Sun Li. Vera added a glowing account—somewhat dramatized—of the panda's quick actions to save von Beaverpelt's life. She wrapped up with an optimistic note: Surely the mystery was soon to be solved. There was no need for Shady Hollow to worry. Justice would be served.

Vera put the finishing touches on the article and then ran to the newsroom with minutes to spare. The copy rabbits took her piece with evident relief. Vera always came in under deadline, true. But try telling that to a rabbit charged with typesetting a special edition with BW Stone breathing down their neck! The big empty space reserved for Vera's article had been looking quite bleak in the past few moments.

"Thank you!" the rabbit squeaked. Rabbits are always polite, even those in a hurry. "Now please get out of my way!"

Vera stepped aside nimbly and went to find BW. He was pacing on top of his desk again, like a tiny general in front of a largely indifferent army.

"Vixen!" he yelled when he saw her. "Get in here!"

"I *am* in here," Vera said. "I just gave the article to the copy editor."

"Good! We'll sell out if the headline is snappy." He spread his paws as if seeing the words plastered outside a building. "I'm thinking 'Murderer Still at Large!' Or 'Killer Runs Amok!'"

"'Killer Runs Amok'?" Vera repeated incredulously.

"'*Vicious Serial* Killer Runs Amok,'" BW amended. "Too long?"

"Stop this nonsense, BW. You don't need to frighten folks into buying papers."

"I'm just trying to put food on the table, fox." BW put on a mournful face. "Like a good provider."

She shook her head. "I'm running down another lead tonight. I should have something interesting to report tomorrow," Vera said.

BW perked up instantly and demanded to know what it was.

"Want to find out? Buy a paper!" Vera skipped out, hearing the scream of "Viiiixen!" as she darted away.

Her good humor fled as she emerged into the brisk evening air. Lenore had been right. Tonight's meeting could be dangerous. But Vera knew that it was also the best chance to find out what was going on. It might be von Beaverpelt himself, trying to meet with her away from the watchful eyes of his family. Did he have to sneak out of his own house to have an honest conversation? Vera hoped life in the von Beaverpelt home was not that terrifying.

As she walked down the street, she saw a surprising figure. "Lefty!" she called. "Is that you?"

The raccoon jumped at hearing his name, looking both startled and guilty. Perhaps if he didn't always *look* guilty, he'd have fewer problems around the Hollow. "Oh, Vixen. It's you."

"I thought Orville said you could stay in jail," she said, once she got close enough to talk at a lower volume.

"Orville did," Lefty noted mournfully. "But then the chief showed up again. *He* kicked me out. Said I was freeloading off the citizens, what with all those catered meals and that nice down mattress!"

"Well, aren't you glad you're not a murder suspect?"

"Rather be a suspect than a victim, if you take my meaning."

"I don't. What are you talking about?"

Lefty glanced around, then leaned in to whisper, "I sometimes get in a bit over my head, fox. I need a bit of cash, so I do a job. I don't ask about the details, you see. I don't get paid to ask questions. Some questions don't want answers, you see."

Vera wanted to scream. Another beast who was afraid of the answers! "I'm not afraid to ask questions, Lefty. What job are you talking about? What did you do that makes you think the murderer might come after you?"

"I can't tell you," he said. "No offense, Vixen, but you're not really the sort to understand. If I'm wrong, then it'll all blow over. But if I'm right . . . well, I'll hightail it out of the Hollow altogether, just you wait and see!"

Before Vera could stop him, Lefty did hightail it. He dashed down a side street toward the river, and Vera knew she'd never catch up to him.

"Maybe they should have kept you in jail," she murmured, turning Lefty's strange half confession over in her mind.

After the odd conversation with Lefty, Vera returned home to her den. She had agreed with Lenore that they would head to the oak stand separately, so as not to spook whoever was meeting Vera there.

It was full dark when Vera left the den again, about an hour before midnight. The oak stand was not particularly close to town; it would take a bit of walking to get there. Fortunately, Vera had excellent night vision and found a well-traveled path. Once out of town, however, the way quickly became less clear. The path narrowed to the width of a single paw, and the silence of the forest made Vera look around far more often than she usually might.

The leaves of the taller canopy obscured the stars, and the moon had already set. Below the branches, it was very dark indeed. The few nocturnal creatures who would normally be about had found reasons to stay in during the past week. No beast wanted to cross paths with a killer. Once, a rustling in the bushes off the path caused Vera to jump, but whatever creature made the noise never appeared. Perhaps it had been just as startled as Vera.

Eventually Vera crossed a mossy log bridge over a stream and found herself at the stand of oaks known for miles around as the oldest and tallest in the forest. Behind the stand, the land sloped sharply upward to the top of a hill, now completely shrouded in darkness. At night the trees seemed sinister, looming over the forest. Vera couldn't see any other creature about, so she sat down on a convenient log and waited.

The woods were quiet. Even the humming of night insects came low to her pointed ears. She thought she heard a sound behind her, far away, near the top of the hill, but when she squinted upward, she could see nothing.

Again, she settled down to wait. Von Beaverpelt—if it was von Beaverpelt—had not yet appeared. Vera had almost resolved to give up and return to the comfort of her den when she heard a real sound behind her. A rustling, a rolling, a rumbling . . . and then a shriek from the sky. From above, Lenore's voice screamed, "Look out!"

Vera swung around to see a huge boulder barreling down the slope. She was directly in its path! For a moment she froze with pure animal fear. But then, as the stone rushed toward her, she sprang to the side with all her might. She felt a jarring pain. The world, already dark, went black.

Chapter 18

"Vera!" a voice called, as if from very far away. "Vera! Can you hear me?"

The fox blinked slowly. Her head ached, and she opened her eyes to find that she was lying on her back at the foot of the hill. Lenore was bent over her, looking worried.

"I don't feel so good," Vera said.

"Of course you don't!" the raven said. "You were out cold!" Vera tried to get up, but it was far too difficult. Her head spun.

"Don't move!" Lenore squawked. "You shouldn't walk. I have to get help!" She looked around at the dark forest. "But I can't leave you! Who knows if the creature who did this is just waiting for me to fly away . . . ?"

"I can defend my—" Vera began to say.

"Ha! My left wing, you can defend yourself! You can barely speak." Lenore rose into the air, fluttering uncertainly. "It's just too far. Even if I fly all the way there, help can't fly back. You'd be all alone for an hour at least."

"I'll get up in a moment."

"You won't if I have anything to say about it."

As Lenore argued, a shadow passed over them.

Lenore cawed loudly in recognition. "It's Heidegger. Professooooor!" she called, flying straight upward in an effort to catch the fast-moving silent bird. "Professor!"

Heidegger checked his flight, tumbling over in midair to circle around the frantic raven. "Whoooo calls?" he asked.

"Help—Vera—big rock—hurt!" was all that Lenore could get out. "Police!"

Heidegger took one glance down at the forest floor, and his huge yellow eyes seemed to take every detail in. The darkness hid nothing from him.

"I'll fetch the bear posthaste!" he hooted. In a moment he had wheeled again, caught an updraft, and angled toward Shady Hollow.

Lenore dropped back down to the ground. "The owl is getting help. Stay strong, Vera."

Vera did her best, but it was hard to concentrate. The pain in her head was soon joined by her aching muscles, which were bruised from her close encounter with the boulder. She had no idea how much time went by before they heard a crashing sound coming toward them.

"It's Orville," Lenore said softly. "He must have run the whole way."

Indeed, the great bear was panting when he skidded to a stop beside Vera and Lenore.

"What happened?" he growled, looking fiercely at the supine figure of the fox.

"It wasn't her fault," Lenore began to explain.

"I didn't say it was!" Orville said. "I asked what happened."

"I was sitting on the fallen beech trunk," Vera said, her voice coming out rather weak. "All of a sudden, Lenore—who was flying above—called out a warning. That boulder rolled all the way down. I'd have been crushed if she hadn't seen it."

Behind Orville, the owl fluttered silently down, saying, "That boulder has been at the top of the hill since . . . well, forever."

"Until tonight," Orville said, squinting up the slope. "I can't see too well in the dark, Professor. Would you mind?"

The owl saluted with one wing. "Always glad to provide assistance to the law!" He took off again, beginning with an awkward run, but soon was gliding upward to the crest of the hill. He was lost in the murk of the forest for a few long moments, but then he sailed back down, following the path of the boulder.

"As I suspected. There is a long branch with markings on each end consistent with being used as a lever. Furthermore, some of the earth was cleared away in the path of the boulder. There was only one way that rock would tumble down . . . directly toward the fallen beech."

"No question about it," the bear said grimly. "That boulder didn't fall by accident."

Vera waited for the inevitable next words, but Orville just looked at her. "You need to be taken back to Shady Hollow, Miss Vixen. A doctor should examine those wounds."

"I shall find Mr. Sun," Heidegger offered before anyone said anything. "I'll tell him to meet you at Miss Vixen's den."

Orville nodded. "That will do."

"I'll fly there to open the door," Lenore said, not waiting for an answer before she took off, too.

Vera and Orville were alone. "You haven't asked why I'm here," she began.

"Not yet, but I will. Count on it, fox." Without another word, the bear bent down and picked Vera up as though she weighed no more than a mouseling.

"You're going to carry me the whole way?" Vera asked, incredulous, and also rather shy.

Orville nodded his massive head. "You're not walking on your own paws, that's for sure."

Remembering their recent argument and her conviction that the police bears were nearly useless, Vera suddenly felt heat in her face. Thank stars her fur was already red! "Thank you," she said.

"Don't mention it," he replied, starting to walk. "And definitely don't write about it in the paper."

Vera would have laughed if she felt better. She'd die of embarrassment before reporting that she had been carried all the way home by Orville.

Sun Li was waiting when they arrived at Vera's den. Orville put Vera down gently, and the panda examined her, checking for broken bones or bleeding. He bandaged a bump on her head, then recommended that Vera rest as long as she could. She did not need stitches and should recover nicely.

Lenore, who had been fretting the whole time, was almost limp with relief and thanked the panda profusely.

Sun Li left then, reminding them all to let Vera sleep.

Orville hadn't left yet. He'd obviously been waiting to ask a few questions. "All right, then. What were you both doing out there so late at night?"

After Vera gave her a quick nod, Lenore explained briefly about the note and the potential lead on the story.

"But it seems someone invited me there to get me out of the way," Vera concluded. She had a suspicion it might have been von Beaverpelt himself. Perhaps he wasn't as sick as he claimed.

"Any idea who?" Orville asked.

Lenore spread her wings. "It's not the time for an in-depth interrogation! Vera's barely coherent, and it's late. How about you come by again tomorrow?"

"Yes," Vera agreed. "I need to rest before I think of all that again."

"Very well," Orville said. He gave the fox a long look as he prepared to depart. "You take a lot of risks, Vixen." Then he left.

"I'm not sure if that was a warning or not."

"Sounded a bit like a backpawed compliment to me," said Lenore.

Vera wondered if she was getting a little too close to figuring out the identity of the murderer. If Lenore had not been there to warn her about the boulder, things could have turned out much differently. Vera closed her eyes.

"We can talk it over in the morn . . ."

She was asleep before she finished the word.

Chapter 19

The whole town was buzzing the next morning. The special edition of the *Herald* had gone out and was being snapped up right and left. News of the attack on Vera was also making the rounds, fueled in part by a chance remark by Heidegger around dawn. Joe could hardly keep up with coffee orders as the café filled up with creatures wanting to know the latest news.

Lenore had spent the night at Vera's in case she needed anything. Vera had had a fairly comfortable night but awoke with a tremendous headache, which was not a surprise to anyone.

"Sun Li left some medicine for you." Lenore indicated a small bottle on Vera's nightstand. "Just take one; they might make you a little woozy."

Vera shook her head. "The only medicine I want is some of Joe's coffee. Let's head over there and hear the gossip."

"If you think you're strong enough."

"I am, thanks to you," she said to Lenore as the raven fussed and straightened things on the dresser. "You saved my life."

"I was so scared," the raven whispered. "I don't know what I would do without you. You're my best friend."

Vera sniffed loudly, but then she recovered. "We have got to catch this killer," she declared, peering into the mirror. "Bandages are not a good look for me, and I am starting to take things personally."

The two made their way to Joe's. Most creatures inside looked curiously at Vera, but, as was usual woodland courtesy, no one made a fuss.

Vera looked around. She was surprised to see Esmeralda von Beaverpelt sitting alone in a booth. "Let's go and join her," Vera whispered.

"Ugh. Why? There are a few empty booths left."

"Yes, but the empty booths won't have any information on how von Beaverpelt's recovery is going."

"You're always on the job, aren't you?" Lenore muttered. But she allowed Vera to steer her toward the booth in question.

"May we join you?" Vera asked in her mildest, least reporterish tone. She made sure to tip her head to show off the bandage.

Esme blinked in surprise. "Why . . . of course."

The two creatures settled in just as a waitress—a dark-furred mink named Lucy—glided over.

"Glad to see you on your paws, Vera," she said. "The usual?"

"Yes, thanks," Vera said.

"Just coffee for me," Lenore added.

The waitress nodded. She walked back to the kitchen and yelled, "Sunny on a slab, hold the snow . . . and a blonde with sand!"

"Coming right up," Joe said cheerfully.

"You're getting a fried egg on toast, no salt," Esme said to Vera. "And Lenore is having coffee with cream and sugar. I've been learning all the jargon," she added.

"Been spending a lot of time at Joe's lately?" Lenore asked.

"Better than spending time at home. With the pater sick in bed, it's a little too crowded."

"Sorry to hear that," Vera murmured.

"Besides, I like the blueberry muffins," Esme said. From the way her eyes moved, it was clear she was also fascinated by the servers who worked the busy morning shift. She commented, "That mink slinks around the joint like *she* owns it instead of Joe."

"Lucy?" Vera asked. "Yeah, she's got an attitude."

"What would it be like," Esme wondered out loud, "to *take* orders all day instead of give them? To have to stand on your paws and never sit?"

"You could get hired and find out," Lenore said, with no expectation that the highfalutin Esme would actually do so.

"I could try," Esme mused.

Vera thought it would be good for her. At Joe's, the servers all grinned as they worked, and they exchanged jokes with the customers. And the money was good. Esme watched avidly as the tips piled up (she was skilled at counting money on the fly).

Then Vera glanced out the window to see Ruby Ewing making her way down the street.

"Look." She nudged Lenore. "Wonder where she came from. Looks like she just woke up."

Esme followed their glances outside. Her gaze narrowed. "That horrible sheep! Mother can't stand her, you know."

Vera could guess why. Ruby's indiscretions were well known. Reginald von Beaverpelt's were less well known, but his name had been linked to Ruby's a few times.

As a beaver wife with ever-growing teeth and a lot of suppressed rage to deal with, Edith had knocked out quite a few masterpieces on that sheep's account. She'd won the ice-sculpture contest at the Hollow's Winter Carnival this past year, and Vera suspected it was almost entirely due to Reginald being out on "unexpected business" for much of the autumn.

It had been a spectacularly intricate ice sculpture, depicting Edith's two daughters in incredible detail. Vera wrote a whole story about it.

The prize for first place turned out to be a beautiful scarf.

A *woolen* scarf. Donated by Ruby.

Vera had added that detail without comment, but she'd always wondered what had happened to the scarf.

Talk about a motive for poisoning Reginald. Maybe life in the von Beaverpelt mansion was more dangerous than she'd thought.

The food came then, and Vera worked to steer the topic of conversation carefully so that Esme would mention things without feeling she was being interrogated.

Esme sighed when the check came. "I suppose I should head home. Mother doesn't like it when we're not accessible."

"Your father may need your assistance, though you say he is recovering nicely."

"This morning he said he couldn't wait to get up," Esme reported. "I think he wants to get back to work."

"He's very dedicated," Lenore said, crumpling her napkin. Vera knew what Lenore was thinking: Reginald couldn't wait to get out of the house and away from his wife!

So Vera offered to walk Esme home. "I'd like to finish that conversation with your dad, and it's not too far out of the way of the police station, where I have to go next. Orville has a few questions for me after last night, anyway," Vera said.

"It is true that he carried you back from the forest?" Esme asked.

"Um, yes," Vera said. *Who let that bit of gossip out?* she wondered.

Esme giggled. "That's so romantic."

"It didn't feel romantic in the least. I mostly just hoped he wouldn't drop me." In fact, Vera never once felt that Orville might drop her—he was too strong for that to be a danger. But still. Romantic? Absolutely not!

They left Joe's. Lenore had to open the bookstore, so Vera and Esme walked along Forest Avenue toward the posh neighborhood of Maple Heights. The von Beaverpelt mansion crowned the whole area with its gracious size and understated elegance.

Along the way, Vera continued to press Esme for details of what might have happened to Otto and to her father.

Esme had a theory Vera had never heard before. "I'm not even sure it happened at all. Otto's death was sad, but was it actually *murder*?"

"Poison was found in that bottle. And a knife was in his back."

Esme only shook her head. "Surely it was all a misunderstanding. And even if Otto *was* murdered, it doesn't mean Daddy was poisoned. I bet he simply had a bad reaction to his breakfast or something. Or he just wanted some attention. He's been grumbling about money more than usual lately. Mother hates that. She says it's gauche."

At the house, they briefly greeted Edith and Anastasia, then headed upstairs to the senior von Beaverpelts' bedroom. "Daddy, are you awake?" Esme called, opening the door. "Miss Vixen is here. She has some questions—"

On seeing an empty bed, Esme stopped momentarily but quickly recovered. "Daddy? Are you feeling better? Where are you?"

No answer was forthcoming.

"What's going on? Where's your father?" Edith demanded, rushing into the room, followed by Anastasia.

"Not in bed where we left him this morning."

"Oh, no!" Edith exclaimed. "How alarming!"

Esme didn't appear alarmed. "He must have felt well enough to go into work for a few hours. You know how he hates not knowing what is happening at the mill every moment of the day."

"He shouldn't be out and about until he's better," Edith fretted.

"Oh, Mother. Let him do what he wants." Anastasia was about to usher Vera out of the room when a shriek from her mother stopped her.

"His watch! He'd never leave for work without his pocket watch!"

Stasia rolled her eyes. "Shall I bring it to him?"

"Do that, and make sure he's all right. Make him come home if he's at all feverish!"

"Yes, Mother." Stasia took the watch and left the house, accompanied by Vera, who jumped at the chance to interview the other daughter. They walked briskly down to the sawmill, which took about ten minutes. The sun was bursting all over after the cloudy morning, so one could almost forget all the unpleasantness of the past week.

They'd just reached the entrance of the main building when Howard Chitters hurried out. He stopped short at seeing Vera and Stasia.

"Miss von Beaverpelt!" he squeaked. "Do you have instructions from your father?"

"What?" Stasia said blankly. "I thought Father was *here*. I'm bringing his watch to him." She held it up.

"No, no, no," Chitters insisted. "He's not been here at all. I was just leaving to call on him at home."

"He's not there, either," she said.

Vera put up a paw. "He may be there after all. Remember, your mother scarcely checked to see, and the house is very large. Perhaps he was still home or in the gardens."

"I suppose he might've been," Stasia amended. "Let's go make sure."

The three returned along the same path. Stasia tried to make awkward conversation as they went, mostly about the state of the Chitters brood.

Howard answered with a distracted air; he was worried about his boss. "It's not like him to be out of touch!"

Their return to the house sparked a full-scale search for von Beaverpelt. He was not found in the house, nor in the greenhouse, nor in the garden. Edith grew more frantic as time went on, though nothing was disturbed. It was as if the lumber magnate had simply walked away.

After Edith had a nervous fit and wilted onto a chaise longue in the living room, Vera suggested the worst possibility.

"He may have started walking to the mill and collapsed somewhere, especially if he overestimated his recovery. Let's enlist some help and find him."

Howard ran back and told the sawmill workers to check the town to find von Beaverpelt. The workers were happy to leave off their regular tasks and go on this special mission, but they sensed that something was wrong. Very wrong. The president of the company should have been located without any trouble. How could von Beaverpelt disappear? He *was* Shady Hollow.

The businesses were checked quickly, and Orville (on hearing the news) joined the hunt as well. A swallow was soon persuaded to make a circuit of the town by air. He did so and finished by soaring over the pond. He saw nothing out of the ordinary except for a strange object on the western shore. He swooped down to look and saw—quite improbably—a pair of striped silk pajamas dangling from a branch. How very odd.

The swallow was just about to fly back to report the incident when he caught a glimpse of something below the surface of the pond. An involuntary squawk exploded from the swallow, and he lost no time in escaping the horror of the scene. He flew back as fast as his wings could carry him.

"Von Beaverpelt! Drowned! Pajamas!" was all he wheezed out before fainting in front of Orville.

Vera overheard the words and winced. "Not again," she said softly.

A contingent of creatures led by the frantic von Beaverpelt

ladies followed the bird's directions to Reginald's final bathing spot. There was the beaver, lying in the water just like Otto before him.

"Oh, my stars!" Chitters said over and over. "What shall we do?"

Vera stared at the horrific scene, her brain momentarily overwhelmed. What was happening to Shady Hollow?

Chapter 20

"Back up!" Orville yelled. "Everyone back up! Don't disturb the body!"

By now the scene was chaos. Mrs. von Beaverpelt and both her daughters had thrown themselves over the prone body of Reginald, which was still soaking wet after being pulled up onto the bank. Then Edith began to wail and rock back and forth in grief. It took an entire regiment of squirrels to pull her off her husband. The daughters were sobbing and wringing their paws.

Lenore and Gladys were kind enough to shepherd the surviving von Beaverpelts back to their mansion to calm down, both hovering over the distraught beavers, using their wings to keep them moving.

After the scene calmed down, Orville managed to find a plank and to put von Beaverpelt's body on it. With the assistance of a few other creatures, he got the body to the police station. Vera took a good look at the crime scene, including the strange sight of the silk pajamas. She took several pictures and then hurried after the group that carried the body.

When she arrived at the police station, she found Orville in shock, staring at none other than Chief Meade, who sat behind his desk as if it was a common thing to do.

"What are you doing here?" Orville asked the chief, forgetting that the chief ought to be there every day.

"I'm working! There's a murder to solve."

"There are two," Orville corrected. "I just fished von Beaverpelt out of the pond."

"Von Beaverpelt! Oh, my."

Orville and the others carried the plank to an empty cell, where Orville gently transferred the body to a cot. When he passed the other cell, he suddenly halted. "Where's Lefty?"

"I let him go. You said there was no evidence to keep him."

"You let him *go?*"

"Yes," the chief said testily. "If he gets up to more mischief, we'll just haul him in again."

"Mischief? Like the murder of von Beaverpelt?"

"We don't know he did that!"

Orville was clearly close to losing his temper. "You let Lefty out of jail, and this afternoon von Beaverpelt is dead!"

The chief blanched. "I say . . . that's most circumstantial . . ."

But it was too late. The other creatures who had helped carry the body over now fled, ready to spread the latest news far and wide. Vera scrawled her own notes in a hasty way, putting the exact quotes on paper before she could forget them.

"Miss Vixen," Orville said, focusing on her, "I think you had better leave. This is official police business."

For once, Vera didn't argue. She caught a certain look in the bear's eye and recognized that this time he would not accept anything other than complete obedience.

———

Orville watched the fox go, sure she was already composing a damning article exposing both him and Meade as incompetents. He was completely shattered; if only he had been able to catch the murderer by now, this would never have happened. Once again he had the unhappy task of summoning the funeral home, this time to take away the beaver's lifeless body. An autopsy would have to be performed first, although, from the large wound on von Beaverpelt's head, it seemed clear that this was no accident.

Once Orville's shock began to wear off, his police brain started to work again. Was the raccoon's fear about being in danger all an act? Where was Lefty now? Was there any hope of catching him again?

Orville sent several pigeons to neighboring towns with instructions to watch out for Lefty. If he turned up in a village, one of Orville's colleagues would let him know. He doubted it would do any good, since Lefty was probably hiding out in the woods somewhere.

Beyond the borders of the small towns that dotted the landscape, the forest quickly turned wild. Sensible creatures do not venture too far into the woods without some protection. Caves can hide a number of uncivilized beasts, and paths often dwindle, leaving one completely lost.

Some folks, like Lefty, use these facts to their advantage. Raccoons are excellent at creating hiding places, some hideouts so skillfully made that one can sit on its roof without even knowing. Orville hoped he wouldn't have to take his investigation into the wild parts of the forest. It was dangerous enough to make even a bear think twice.

For her part, Vera was as shocked as Orville. Reginald von Beaverpelt was dead! How could this be? The entire town of Shady Hollow was stunned. Otto's death was sad. But the beaver was one of their most well-known and respected citizens, and now he had been brutally murdered.

Although Vera was shaken, she tried to stay calm and picture the scene in her mind again. There had to be a clue somewhere.

Sometime later there came a soft knock on her front door. Vera opened her eyes and called out, "Just a minute."

When she unlocked the door, she was pleased to see Lenore and invited her in, offering to make some tea.

"I see you finally put a lock on your door," Lenore said.

"Well, it's the fashion now," Vera said, wishing it were not.

After a moment, Vera stopped fussing with the teapot and looked steadily at her friend.

"If only he had been able to talk to me the other day," she lamented. "Von Beaverpelt knew something, and I think he was trying to warn me about someone, but his family wouldn't let him talk to me. If only I had tried harder."

Lenore shushed her, saying, "You can't blame yourself, Vera. You've been putting yourself in danger to solve a case the police can't figure out. The only creature to blame for this whole horrible mess is the murderer. You will figure it out, but you have to be careful."

Vera knew her friend was right. She was a reporter, after all, not a detective. She had already gone above and beyond what was expected of her. The happenings in Shady Hollow had to come to an end. She would be happy to go back to reporting big news like a new flavor of coffee at Joe's Mug or Professor Heidegger's latest dull lecture.

But for now, murder remained on the front page.

Chapter 21

Throughout Shady Hollow, there was talk about Lefty's absence, but most of this was eclipsed by discussion of von Beaverpelt's murder and what it meant for the town.

"Edith von Beaverpelt is technically in charge now, but she has no idea how to run the mill. Shady Hollow is doomed" was a common refrain over the next few days.

But such gossip was whispered, not shouted. The von Beaverpelts were still the most powerful family around.

Everyone was planning to attend the funeral, which promised to be a much bigger affair than Otto Sumpf's simple service. Edith and her daughters were pulling out all the stops, and none of the townsfolk wanted to miss the spectacle. Of course they were shocked and saddened by the death of such a prominent citizen, but you couldn't discount the entertainment value.

Reginald von Beaverpelt's funeral was to be held at Shady Hollow Church after the deceased was privately interred in the family plot at the cemetery (a custom particular to beavers). Parson Conkers, the only clergy in town, had naturally agreed to officiate at the family service and was thus the only non–von Beaverpelt at the actual burial.

In contrast, the public event was packed with almost every creature in town by the time Vera and Lenore arrived. Vera had spent half the morning trying on hats to find one that would cover the bandage on her head. She was unsuccessful and almost made them late in the bargain. They were dressed somberly and appropriately in black, but Vera still had a large white bandage on her head. Oh, well.

All the beasts wore their best outfits, but it was the von Beaverpelt widow and her daughters who had really outdone themselves. Edith was swathed in an enormous black cape that covered her from head to paw. She also sported an elaborately feathered black hat with heavy netting that obscured her face from view. Her daughters were similarly attired, and all three carried large black pawkerchiefs. The sobbing and wailing coming from the front pew quieted slightly when Parson Dusty took his place behind the pulpit at the front of the church.

Vera and Lenore found seats in one of the back pews just as the parson cleared his throat.

"Dear friends," he began, "once again we are gathered under sad circumstances. Today we must bid farewell to one of our finest citizens who was taken from us too soon. Reginald von Beaverpelt was president of the sawmill here in the Hollow and was one of our most generous and respected neighbors. He leaves behind his loving wife, Edith, and two beautiful daughters, Anastasia and Esmeralda."

At this, there was louder sobbing from the family pew and some violent coughing from some of the other areas of the sanctuary. Dusty quelled this disturbance with a sharp glance and continued with his eulogy.

"Reginald von Beaverpelt was not always the pillar of the community that y'all are familiar with," the jackrabbit said. "He was once Reggie Pelt, a young tough beaver from a poor area of the forest, determined to better his situation in life. After years of hard work, he built an empire and transformed himself into Reginald von Beaverpelt, a scion of industry. But he was also a husband and a father. He will be greatly missed in the community, as well as at home. And I say to you again . . . we must find justice for this creature. We can't let his murderer go unpunished!"

Parson Dusty was getting a little carried away at this point; he began pounding on the pulpit to emphasize his point. There was some muttering from the family pew, and Parson Dusty recovered his composure. "Thank y'all for coming. A reception will be held at the mansion."

Edith and her daughters filed out of the church in a dignified manner. Everyone else followed after them in a mad dash. None of the townsfolk wanted to miss out on seeing the von Beaverpelt mansion. The family generally did not entertain nor open their home to their humbler neighbors. They were the closest the woodland had to royalty. No animal wanted to miss this opportunity to see how royalty lived.

Both Joe and Sun Li had been asked to prepare food for the funeral; there were simply too many guests for one place to manage everything. The servers from Joe's were moonlighting as caterers, going around the rooms with fresh trays of mini–vegetable rolls.

Most townsfolk stood around the elaborate rooms at the von Beaverpelt mansion and gawked at the furnishings. Shady Hollow residents lived quite simply, with only a few possessions and plain furniture. Life at the von Beaverpelt home was quite different. The furniture was antique and fancy, and lovely patterned silk rugs lay in every room. Oil paintings with heavy gold frames adorned the walls. Most seemed to be portraits of von Beaverpelt ancestors.

Vera nudged Lenore. "Who are all these wealthy relatives? Parson Dusty said von Beaverpelt came from a poor background."

Lenore shrugged and took another nibble of her mini–vegetable roll. "It looks like maybe Reginald married into money instead of making it on his own."

"Edith is the one with the family wealth?" Vera asked.

"She must be. That could certainly be the reason he never wanted to divorce her," Lenore said. "Maybe it was even why he married her in the first place."

Vera mulled this over while she took a sip of her plum wine and cast an eye around the room. Most creatures had cozied up to the open bar and were loosening up. When Vera caught her boss's eye, BW Stone gave her a wink, suggesting there would be plenty of news to report if she plied drunken creatures for information. She pretended not to notice and looked away.

Vera and Lenore were standing off to one side and observing the room, which was quite a din of animal chatter and clinking glasses.

A scream broke through: "Get out!"

All the townsfolk turned to stare at the front door.

Standing just inside, looking as much like a widow as Edith von Beaverpelt herself, was Ruby Ewing. There was a low murmur from the guests and then another shriek as the widow von Beaverpelt advanced toward the newcomer.

"Just what do you think you are doing here, you woolly homewrecker?" bellowed Edith, her voice rising on every syllable until the last word was delivered at an almost-impossible volume. The feathers on her hat wobbled with the strength of her emotion. Her daughters were standing on either side of her in a demonstration of family solidarity.

"This is a gathering of our papa's family and friends," added Stasia, moving toward Ruby while Esme comforted their mother. "You are neither. Please leave."

Ruby stood her ground, and Vera wondered if things were going to get physical. Then she saw Joe standing by the door, looking ready to break up any further altercation. On the other side of the room, Orville slowly moved through the crowd. If there was a fight, it would not last long.

But Ruby didn't move.

"I loved him, too," mumbled Ruby in such a low voice that Vera barely caught it, and then the sheep turned and went out the way she came.

Joe heaved a noisy sigh of relief. He cast a look around, then hurried out the door as well, presumably to see if Ruby was all right; she had worked for Joe in the past, and he knew her better than most townsfolk.

After he left, the crowd's chattering picked up again, fueled by alcohol and gossip.

Edith was spent from her emotional outburst, and the girls took her upstairs to rest in her bedroom. Then, after a little freshening up, Stasia and Esme came back downstairs to their guests. Servers continued working the room, and the guests were very glad to have something safe to talk about.

The face-off between Edith and Ruby was the highlight of the afternoon, though.

One by one, the townsfolk finished their drinks, wrapped up a few treats in napkins, and prepared to take their leave. Soon the vast living room was almost empty, with the exception of Vera, Lenore, the servers, and Sun Li, who was clearing away the few leftover trays.

Vera and Lenore had exhausted all their leads (and themselves) and decided to go. First, however, they approached Stasia and Esme to express their condolences. The beaver heiresses were not exactly gracious, but they did thank the fox and the raven for coming. Vera had a few more questions, but it had been a long and emotional day for everyone, so she kept them to herself.

As Lenore and Vera headed for home, Vera said to her friend, "While you were getting a refill on your wine and talking to Gladys, Orville came over to talk to me."

"Did he ask for your alibi?"

"No. He asked me if we could get together tomorrow and compare notes about the case!"

Lenore shook her head. "The police must be desperate to solve this case if they're asking the press for help."

Vera frowned, but Lenore went on. "You know what I mean. Orville has kept you out of it so far."

"That's what I thought," Vera agreed. "Still, I couldn't turn the offer down. So I said yes. We're meeting at the station early tomorrow morning."

Chapter 22

The next day Vera awoke early and went over her notes on each suspect and their alibi. She had not slept well. She had nightmares about the boulder hitting her and how close she had come to being killed herself. She stopped at Joe's for coffee before meeting Orville at the police station.

At that early hour, Joe's Mug was deserted, with the exception of Joe, who was brewing coffee and setting out fresh pastries.

"Some event yesterday," Joe said. "I wondered if even that mansion could hold every creature in the Hollow."

"Every creature but Ruby," Vera noted. "Did you speak to her afterward?"

"I did," Joe confirmed. But he said nothing more, and it

was clear that whatever passed between the two creatures had been a private conversation.

Vera wasn't sure what to say about it. While Edith's reaction had been extreme, Ruby's behavior was an open secret, and no one really doubted Edith's accusation.

"May I get two coffees this morning?" she asked, choosing a safe topic.

"Didn't sleep?" Joe said as he poured coffee into two large cups.

"Not much, but that's not why." Vera explained she was meeting Orville, who had complained about the quality of the coffee at the station. Too exhausted for any other gossip, even with Joe, Vera merely paid and hurried on her way.

When Vera arrived at the police station, Orville was there at his desk. He didn't appear to have slept any better than she did. He accepted the large cup of coffee gratefully and invited Vera to take a seat in the visitor's chair across from him.

Vera was interested to see that the police bear was once again studying the autopsy reports of Otto Sumpf and Reginald von Beaverpelt. There was also a complex-looking description of the poison, submitted by Dr. Broadhead.

Vera pulled out her notes, mainly a list of all the possible suspects and their alibis or lack thereof. The residents of Shady Hollow were not used to accounting for their whereabouts at any given time. It didn't help that the exact time of Otto's murder could not be pinpointed beyond "between sunset and sunrise." Most creatures said they'd been at home, naturally, but no one could provide much in the way of verification.

Orville had more notes of his own, including a complete profile on Lefty.

"No success in bringing him back in yet, I assume?" Vera asked.

The bear shook his heavy head. "One thing I'll say for Lefty: he knows how to hide. He could be nearly anywhere in the woodlands at this point."

"But you must have a lead."

"One," he said. "Lefty has a lady friend. I went to her place the day after Lefty was released. She denied seeing him, of course, but I think there's a good chance she knows where he's hiding. I'm having her place watched."

Vera read the information with interest. Lefty's lady, Rhonda, lived in a neat little cottage in Elm Grove, which was a small village farther downriver. According to the report, most of her neighbors liked her, although she was a petty thief much like her beau.

"She did seem shocked by the report of von Beaverpelt's death," Orville said. "I'll wager she didn't know about it. If Lefty told her he'd been arrested for Otto's killing, he didn't say a word about von Beaverpelt."

"It's possible Lefty got out of town before he knew about the death," Vera said. "Assuming he's innocent."

"I can't assume that," Orville growled. "Why else would he leave town so fast?"

"Because he'd be blamed for the next bad thing. Isn't that exactly what happened?"

"Are you saying you don't think Lefty's to blame?"

Vera argued, "He was in jail when von Beaverpelt was poisoned the first time. How could he have done that? And besides, *why* would Lefty kill either Otto or von Beaverpelt? He has no motive."

"You should be his lawyer, Miss Vixen."

"I'm just trying to find out the truth."

"So am I." Orville sat back and sighed. "But nothing makes sense. I'm missing a piece of the puzzle."

So Orville and Vera compared their notes. Vera gnawed on a pencil while she mulled the situation over in her mind. Answers eluded them.

———

After talking over the case with Orville, Vera returned to the cemetery. She didn't have any plan in mind, but she was drawn to the peacefulness of the hill where Shady Hollow's "permanent residents" slept, and she couldn't help but find herself standing over Reginald's grave.

Who had he been, really? Parson Dusty had given such a rousing speech after Otto's death, one that made the townsfolk realize who they had lost. But his eulogy of von Beaverpelt left more questions than answers. Was he born poor, as the parson claimed? Did he get his money through hard work or through marriage, and did it really matter which one? Was Edith's show of grief real or a put-on? And, in the end, who killed him and why?

"Good afternoon, Miss Vixen," a smooth voice said very close beside her.

Vera jumped in surprise. She hadn't heard anyone approach, but now Ruby Ewing, still in mourning wear, stood right next to her.

"Hello, Ruby," she said, hoping her shock wasn't showing. As a fox, Vera wasn't used to anything getting past her. And certainly not a creature like Ruby who had never been known to be subtle.

Ruby was watching her through the mesh of her little veiled hat. "I didn't think you knew Reggie well enough to visit his grave so soon after the funeral."

"Well, I didn't," Vera admitted. "I just came up here . . . for perspective, I guess."

"I see." Ruby nodded. "You don't realize how precious life is until you lose someone, do you?"

"I suppose not." Vera wondered if Ruby had a specific reason for coming to the graveyard. Had she been following Vera? And if so, for how long?

But Ruby only looked down at the freshly turned dirt of the grave. Flowers would be planted soon, but now the ground was bare and ugly, like a scar. "I came to say goodbye to him without an audience."

"Oh! Shall I leave?" Vera offered, expecting Ruby to say yes.

"You don't need to." The sheep sighed. "There's no point in hiding anything now, is there?"

"Hiding?" Vera asked. Was Ruby about to confess something?

"I loved Reggie. I admit it! He loved me, too. He was going to leave Edith, you know. He promised we would start a new life together, somewhere else. He was saving money, keeping it from his wife's prying eyes. He wanted to be sure we'd have enough to be comfortable. Oh, nothing made me happier than the thought of Reggie and me together!

"But then this happened." Ruby sighed again, gesturing to the grave. "My dear Reggie, gone! I can never see him again, or talk to him, or be with him . . ." She sniffed loudly.

"I'm . . . sorry," Vera said. She was unsure of the etiquette when offering condolences to a mistress.

Behind the veil, Ruby's black eyes hardened. "She found out about us, I'm sure. Edith. She couldn't stand the idea of him leaving her, so she did the one thing that would stop him. She killed him!"

"You're saying Edith von Beaverpelt murdered her husband?" Vera asked quietly.

"Of course," Ruby said contemptuously. "Think of it. She was in danger of losing her place as the town's first lady. She would have been disgraced and left poor to boot. No, she knew she'd never convince Reggie to leave me. So she took her revenge. She was the one hovering by his bedside, feeding him poison bit by bit, weakening him for the final blow. Who else had a better opportunity? She had the run of the house and the office if she chose. She hated him at the end because he loved me more!"

"But what about Otto?" Vera asked, though she was troubled to admit that Ruby's story did make a certain amount of sense.

"Poor Otto," Ruby said. "She must have been practicing. To see how much poison a body could take. Otto wasn't the high-powered captain of industry that Reggie was. Who would make a fuss if he died?"

"But Otto was also stabbed," Vera pointed out. Who could forget? The memory of the toad being pulled to the shore of the pond, and the terrible revelation of the knife in his back . . . It had started all of this.

"Who can say what a beaver driven insane with jealousy might do? Let the police ask her what she was thinking. If they have the guts to arrest her! The police are always keen to accuse the powerless. When the upper crust misbehaves—oh, it's a different matter then."

"I'm sure the law treats everyone the same in Shady Hollow," Vera said stiffly. Granted, the law usually did that by ignoring duty altogether and taking fishing trips every day. Chief Meade probably wouldn't dare to arrest Edith. Would Orville?

Ruby laughed. "Oh, fox, you don't have a clue. You wouldn't know. Everyone respects *you*. The hard-working reporter from the big city! *You* haven't been the gossip on every creature's tongue. *You* haven't been turned away at doors where every other creature is welcome."

"Like at the von Beaverpelts' last night?"

"It's just more proof that she hates me and would do anything to hurt me. Even after she killed her own husband."

"This is all fascinating, but there's nothing to prove *you* innocent right now, either. You don't have an alibi. For either death."

"I was with Reggie when poor Otto died!" Ruby blurted out. "I didn't tell the police before because I didn't want to hurt Reggie's name. But now it doesn't matter, does it?"

Vera's journalist heart sparked to life. "You were with von Beaverpelt that night?" She pulled out her notebook and pencil. "Where, exactly?"

"We used to meet in the woods because there was no place in town where we could be together."

"I see," Vera said, scribbling. "And where were you the day Reginald died?"

"I work at the nursing home, you know." Ruby paused. "I was at work at the time Reggie died. Ask them and they'll tell you."

"What are you going to do now?"

"I don't know," said Ruby. "I don't think I can live here any longer. Not when I think of Reggie every day. I may go out west in the spring. It's not too late to start fresh somewhere else."

The sheep looked down at the grave again, and Vera took the cue to get out of the way. She left Ruby grieving on the hilltop. She now had a string of fresh allegations and a lot of work to do.

Chapter 23

Vera made her way out of the cemetery and back to the police station as quickly as she could.

"Orville!" she called as soon as she opened the door. "I have news!"

The police bear looked up from a large map spread out on his desk. "So do I. We found a paw print in the von Beaverpelt home—it belongs to a raccoon! Lefty wasn't at the wake, obviously, so I *need* to find him to get a straight answer as to when he might have left it there. He sure wasn't invited over socially—"

"Orville," Vera broke in. "I just got done talking with Ruby Ewing. She accused Edith von Beaverpelt of both murders!"

Orville was, to say the least, stunned. "Are you sure?" he asked.

"I was hit on the head, but I know what I heard! That's what Ruby said. And she told me her alibi for both murders as well. She says she met Beaverpelt for a tryst on the night Otto died. She wouldn't give his name at the time you asked her about it because she was protecting her lover."

"And during the second murder?"

"She says she was at the nursing home. I'll check out her story right now. But she says Edith killed Reginald rather than see him run off with her."

The deputy looked distressed, his huge paws spread wide. "I can't arrest Edith von Beaverpelt for murder! She's the richest creature in the county."

"Orville!" Vera nearly shouted. "You'll arrest the murderer no matter how rich or poor the creature turns out to be. That's your job."

"Maybe the chief should do it. He's the sort of bear for that detail. Got the shiny badge and all." Privately, Orville couldn't conceive of a jury convicting a wronged beaver wife—especially not a rich one. Orville wondered if the fallout from such a spectacular arrest might even result in Chief Meade's resignation, leading the way for *him* to become chief. He would like that, and surely there would be no more murders to deal with by that point. Shady Hollow would return to the peaceful, friendly town it had always been.

Vera interrupted his imaginings. "We need evidence first. You can't arrest any creature yet."

"Well, I intend to pursue Lefty," Orville said firmly. "Whatever Ruby says, we have a real paw print to explain. I'll be curious to hear how Lefty backs his way out of this one."

Orville found his pair of cuffs in the desk drawer and headed out of the station, Vera at his side. When they reached the newspaper office, she bade Orville luck and went inside.

Time for some good old-fashioned journalism, she decided. It had been a few days since she had spent time in the office. She now had a slew of notes and the story Ruby had confided. What to write for tomorrow's issue?

It was much too early to let any hint of Ruby's accusation go public . . . though she suspected the sheep was secretly hoping the paper would print the allegation immediately. Vera rarely printed anything without statements from two independent sources. She was an old-school journalist, despite her youth. But she still had plenty of material to work with for a story.

Setting a fresh piece of foolscap in the typewriter, the fox got to work. As she wrote, something Ruby mentioned worked its way into Vera's brain. The sheep said von Beaverpelt had been saving money to run away. If what Parson Dusty said at the funeral was also true—that von Beaverpelt had no money of his own—then where did he get the money from?

"Chitters," she muttered. The mouse had been so upset when Vera spoke with him at the sawmill. What had he said? Too much spending . . .

Without another key typed, Vera was off and running.

The sawmill was not operating in observance of the owner's death; all workers had been given a few days' leave after the funeral. Thus, Vera found Howard Chitters at home, looking as overworked as ever.

"Oh, hello, Miss Vixen!" he squeaked when he flung open the door. "How can I help you?" Two mouselings were hanging from his front limbs.

"May we talk for a few moments?" Vera asked, looking askance at the little creatures. "In private?"

"Go find your mother," Chitters ordered his offspring. Within seconds, they vanished.

"My goodness," Vera said.

"My wife is sick today, so she's resting in the bedroom. Well, she *was* resting," Howard corrected himself. "What is this about?"

"What was wrong with the sawmill accounts?" Vera asked bluntly.

Howard looked even more nervous. "Er . . . nothing . . . that is . . ."

"You mentioned something to that effect on the day von Beaverpelt was poisoned at the office." Vera smiled to reassure him. "Look, what if this could help catch the murderer?"

"You're right, I suppose." He went and pulled out the account books—he had brought them home from work—and set them on the table. After brewing a strong pot of tea for both of them, Chitters sat down. Vera pulled out her notebook, with the intention of finding out exactly what was going on.

"I'd been troubled by a number of small errors in the books over the last several months," said Howard. "It wasn't much at first. A few odd payments, a check or two gone missing."

Vera nodded. Such things could happen at a busy place like the sawmill, and Howard surely knew that no business could have 100 percent accurate books. "What made you think twice?"

"It soon became apparent that there was more going on than simple mistakes." He pointed out a column of numbers in red. "A large amount of money was unaccounted for," Howard said.

"What did your boss say?"

"I tried to bring the subject up to Mr. von Beaverpelt several times, but he was always putting me off. 'Don't worry about a few cents, Chitters. We are paying our workers and our suppliers, and that's what matters!' But the discrepancies only grew worse."

The mouse bent over the books, pointing out patterns in page after page of careful entries. Every so often he'd make a note of a particular number or name on a separate sheet of paper.

Both creatures were so absorbed in his work that they didn't hear his wife calling from the bedroom until her voice rattled the china.

"Oh, excuse me!" he said, running to the bedroom. "What is it, my love?"

Vera could hear the conversation.

"Can you heat up some of the spring vegetable soup, dear? I'm famished. What are you working on? I yelled ten times."

"Just something for work, dearest."

Howard reappeared and walked toward the kitchen to make the soup.

Vera used the time to look at the books herself. After careful perusing, she finally noticed something new. Every month, like clockwork, a sum of five hundred dollars was paid to a creature or company with the initials B. S. There was no other indication of who or what B. S. might be.

Howard rejoined her then. "Ah, you saw those payments. I looked at all the names. Everyone the sawmill does business with. No one has those initials."

Vera noticed the last payment was made the week before von Beaverpelt's murder, and there had not been any since then. However, she realized Howard's boss had gone to a lot of trouble to obscure the payments from his diligent accountant. If von Beaverpelt had lived, Howard might never have discovered the payments. He was not suspicious by nature, and he was usually far too busy to make such a comprehensive study of the sawmill's finances.

"We need to bring these books to Orville," Vera said.

"Are you sure? I don't want to sully von Beaverpelt's name."

"But what if this is a clue to the identity of his murderer?"

Howard dithered for a while, wishing that von Beaverpelt was there to tell him what to do. Von Beaverpelt never asked his wife or daughters for advice about business matters, Howard was sure of that much. From this day forward, Howard Chitters would honor the memory of his fallen boss by making his own decisions.

"Very well. But we must go together. The account books are my responsibility."

At that moment, there was another loud call from the bedroom. "Coming, dear," said Howard.

He looked back at Vera. "How about tomorrow morning?"

Since little mouselings were already peeping around the corners of the room, Vera agreed.

"See you then!" she said.

Vera returned to the newspaper office, excited but still overwhelmed.

After typing up her notes for her next article, which focused on Lefty's disappearance and left out any mention of von Beaverpelt's affair, Vera had reached her limit. Despite what she'd learned from Chitters, something was terribly wrong in the evidence that had piled up so far. She couldn't make out precisely what element was missing. Nothing was more frustrating than trying to complete a puzzle with only half the pieces. Logically, once she confirmed a creature's alibi, Vera could cross their name off the list of suspects. Yet this time, the same names kept popping up as possibilities. She had to talk to Lenore.

The bookshop was busy over the lunch hour, with beasts browsing every level of the store. Vera had to wait patiently until Lenore finished ringing up some customers, but she was not feeling patient. She tried to read one of Lenore's featured titles, the translation of the northern thriller *The Squirrel Who Kicked the Hornet's Nest*. Otto Sumpf had been a fan of the series for years, since he could read it in the original language. But Vera couldn't sit still, and the book was soon forgotten on the table beside the chair where she had sequestered herself to wait.

Eventually Lenore had a lull and flew up to see Vera. It was an advantage to have wings when one worked in retail.

"You look perturbed," the raven said.

Vera explained her troubles with the case. "Why can't I seem to really eliminate anyone as a suspect, other than by gut feeling? I need solid evidence, and it all keeps shifting. Take the alibis, for instance. We've done nothing but ask folks where they've been over the past week, and yet we have so little to show for it."

"I've thought about that," Lenore said quietly, since there were still some browsers in the shop. "The problem is the method of the murders. Both victims were poisoned, which means an alibi doesn't really prove much at all. The wine and the coffee could have been prepared well in advance. In von Beaverpelt's case, it seems obvious that some creature planned to get the poisoned beverage into von Beaverpelt's office long before. They might not have really cared exactly when he drank it, as long as he died within a few days. That's why the murderer didn't try again right away when von Beaverpelt survived the first attempt. Our killer waited for their next chance, when von Beaverpelt was alone and couldn't call for help."

"Well, assuming we know the precise time he vanished," Vera added. "All we know for sure is that Edith and her daughters say they saw him in bed that morning—alive—and by noon he was dead in the pond. That's a long gap."

"The murderer could have killed him on the way to the sawmill or on the way back. There were a few hours between the time Edith discovered he was missing and the time his body was found."

Vera threw up her paws in frustration. "How can we narrow it down?"

"Alibis aren't getting you anywhere," Lenore advised. "Try looking for motives instead."

"Otto gave everyone a motive," Vera grumbled.

"That's too easy. Something *made* someone kill Otto, and then von Beaverpelt. Until you can find out why, you won't find the killer."

Lenore had to leave then, since a mouse had a question about *Of Mice & Men*.

"Yes, of course. It's in fantasy," Lenore said, flying over to assist.

Vera sat for a moment afterward, pondering. Motive! Then she leaped up and dashed out of the bookstore. Oddly, considering her profession and her naturally sharp senses, she did not notice she was being watched on her way back home.

Chapter 24

The next day, Vera met Howard Chitters at the police station. The little mouse was laden with large account books.

"Orville," he squeaked, "I have some evidence you need to see." After a long-winded recitation of all his meticulous research, he showed the accounts to Orville. All those lines of numbers meant absolutely nothing to the bear.

"Just tell me what you discovered, Chitters," he growled impatiently.

Vera gave the mouse an encouraging nudge.

Howard looked a little nervous, but he took a deep breath and soldiered on. "Mr. von Beaverpelt was paying some creature monthly from the sawmill account and trying to cover it up."

"Who?" asked the bear.

"Well, it's right here," Howard insisted.

Orville peered at the page where Howard's paw was pointing. "So who the heck is B. S.?"

Howard exhaled noisily. "I don't know, but it's a clue. I thought the police could figure out the rest."

Orville looked over the mouse's head in confusion. "Well, all right. I'll put it in my report," the bear said doubtfully. He took a moment to scratch down Howard's explanation in his ledger, which took longer than it might have because he had to ask a lot of questions to clarify exactly how the books were wrong.

Vera could practically read the bear's thoughts as he worked: *How can this little mouse understand all these numbers?*

Orville finished the report with a sigh of relief. "There. That's done. Since I have you here, Chitters, can you tell me if there have been any break-ins at the sawmill lately? Or if any suspicious characters have been seen lurking about?"

"What makes a character suspicious?" Howard asked, puzzled.

"'Skulking, lurking, stalking, casing the joint, possessing a raccoon-like shape' . . . the usual." In fact, Orville was reciting verbatim from the *Big Book of Policing*.

"No, I can't say I saw Lefty at the sawmill recently." Howard was not an assertive creature, in general. But neither was he a fool. "And no one has reported a break-in or a theft."

"I see." Orville was obviously disappointed.

"So much for easy evidence of Lefty's guilt," Vera noted. "I'm still not convinced he had anything to do with the murders."

"You have your theories, fox. I have mine."

A knock sounded on the doors of the station, and a woodchuck stepped through. It was one of the carpenters from the mill, which was still mostly closed.

"Excuse me for interrupting, Deputy. Mr. Chitters, I went by your home, and your wife said you were here at the station. Mrs. von B is asking for you."

"Really?" Howard looked surprised. "Me in particular?"

"She needs some assistance with the sawmill operations, I gather."

"Oh, dear. Please excuse me." Howard gathered up the account books.

Vera understood his concern. Edith von Beaverpelt was technically his boss now, and she was not a patient creature.

"May I join you?" she asked. "I happen to have a few questions for Edith."

"Chitters, wait outside for a moment," Orville said. "I need to talk to Miss Vixen."

Howard followed the woodchuck out of the station.

Vera turned to Orville. "Don't you dare tell me I can't talk to Mrs. von Beaverpelt. I'm a reporter, and I have a right to—"

"Shush up, fox." Orville held up a paw. "I was just going to tell you to be careful."

"Really?"

"Well, if the sheep is correct about her theory and Edith is a murderer—not that I think it's likely—she might do something violent if you ask the wrong questions. You're smart, Miss Vixen, but you're also pushy. Push a murderer too hard and you might get pushed back. Or worse."

She looked at Orville in surprise. Was the bear actually concerned about her? Or did he really think the danger was so great? Then she remembered the boulder tumbling down the hill and knew he was right.

"I'll be careful," she promised. "The most dangerous thing I'll face at the von Beaverpelt mansion is the protests from tracking mud on those shiny oak floors."

"Good luck," Orville said. "You'll need it."

Vera stepped outside to find Howard waiting alone. "I'm to go directly to the mansion," he said. "Edith hasn't been to the sawmill yet."

So the creatures headed up to the von Beaverpelt mansion rather than the mill.

Edith was pacing in the study when they arrived.

"Oh, thank goodness!" she said when Chitters walked in, paws full of books. "I have so many questions." She saw Vera then and looked less pleased. "What can I do for you, Miss Vixen?"

"I just wanted to ask a few questions in preparation for my article on your husband's illustrious life. But, please, talk with Howard first. I'll sit here quite patiently."

And she did, finding an unobtrusive corner where she could still hear every word.

Edith seemed to forget about her within a few seconds. "Mr. Chitters," she began. "I am concerned."

"About what, ma'am?" he asked, sitting on a taller stool after depositing the account books on a nearby table. The height of the stool just brought him to eye level with the larger creature.

"We must reopen the mill as soon as possible. My husband would have expected nothing less." Edith paused to dab her eyes with a tissue. She was still wearing widow's weeds, of course.

"Very good, ma'am. Go ahead and open it." It was no secret that Howard was looking forward to returning to work. He loved his family, but life in the Chitters home was not exactly quiet.

"But I don't know how!" Edith confessed. "Reggie never talked with me about the business. What if I do everything wrong? We'll go broke if the sawmill fails. I'll go broke." She burst into sobs at that point, stuffing her snout into the tissue.

Howard looked quite terrified at the emotional display.

"Just . . . open it. Send word to the employees that work shall resume tomorrow and notify the suppliers to resume shipments. You'll need to verify that the barges can accommodate our products. They may have taken on other shipments, not knowing how long we'd be closed. Of course, if you want to make up for lost hours, you could offer bonus pay for workers who take an extra shift . . ." Howard paused, seeing Edith's eyes grow big and round as she heard all the instructions.

"How does one go about all that?"

Howard's little pink nose twitched once, in a nervous way. "Well . . . um . . . that is. Do you want me to take care of it?"

"Yes," Edith gasped. "Please. I couldn't possibly cope with it all."

Howard gave a quick little bow. "Don't worry, ma'am. I'll start things off, and you just come down to the mill when you're ready to take over."

He picked up the books and hurried out of the mansion, glad to have a task again.

Edith turned her attention to Vera, who remained seated. "Well, Miss Vixen? What questions do you have about my husband's 'illustrious life'?"

Vera flipped to a fresh page in her notebook. "Just a few points of clarification, ma'am. The record is unclear about Mr. von Beaverpelt's origins. Where did you two meet?"

Though Vera kept her tone casual, Edith didn't relax.

"I don't remember."

"How about a story from your courtship? Something to let readers know how you two fell in love."

"I don't remember," Edith repeated.

"Your wedding day, then," Vera probed. "No lady forgets her wedding day. Did your family attend?"

"Of course they attended! They paid for it, didn't they?" Edith snapped.

"How generous of them. Your gown must have cost a small fortune by itself. I saw the portrait of you wearing it. You know, the one hanging near the fireplace."

"I loved that gown." Edith's voice softened momentarily as she was drawn back into memory. "It was my mother's, and she wanted me to wear it. All those little freshwater pearls at the hem. I thought they were so pretty . . ."

"I'm sure your mother was delighted to see you in it. Tell me about the wedding. It must have been quite the affair!"

"*Affair,*" Edith echoed. Her expression hardened. "I don't think I will, Miss Vixen. I'm not particularly keen on sharing all the family *affairs* with the press."

Vera could have kicked herself for her clumsy choice of words. "Well," she hedged, "I'm not asking you to tell any secrets."

"You'd better not, fox. I'm not pleased when others pry into my business." The widow leaned forward, her eyes narrow. "Those who tangle with me soon regret it. Do I make myself clear?"

"Yes, ma'am." Vera knew when to end an interview. "I'll see myself out."

"See that you do."

Vera exited as quickly as possible. So Edith von Beaverpelt had a streak of command as strong as her late husband's. Maybe she'd been the one to teach him how to deliver a threat. Maybe she'd lost her patience when Reginald got ideas of his own.

In any case, Vera wouldn't get any more information from Edith. But she did seem like a prime suspect.

Chapter 25

While Vera and Howard were meeting with the new head of the sawmill, Orville addressed the matter of the mysterious raccoon paw print found inside the mansion. He took it upon himself to search out Lefty once and for all.

In truth, Orville didn't expect it to be such a big problem to find Lefty. After all, Lefty hadn't even wanted to leave the jail cell the first time; Chief Meade had to throw him out. Orville wondered if Lefty had been using some sort of reverse psychology on him. Maybe Lefty wasn't a goof but rather an evil genius!

A moment of recollection brought Orville back to reality. This was Lefty, after all. The raccoon once managed to lock himself *inside* the bank during a robbery and then had to call the police for help getting out.

Still, Orville was taking no chances. Lefty had definitely been in the von Beaverpelt mansion, and von Beaverpelt was definitely dead. Orville didn't need any more facts than those at the moment. He wanted Lefty back in jail.

Orville strolled around town, peeking into Lefty's usual haunts. He was not at his place of residence, a room he let from a widowed rat who ran a boardinghouse down on the bank of the river. Orville asked after Lefty, but the landlady hadn't seen him for a couple days.

"Not unusual, you know," she said. "Lefty mostly sleeps all day and goes out all night." She gave Orville's shiny badge a significant glance. "I expected to see you sooner! You must have a few questions for him, Officer."

Orville had many, but as the day went on, it seemed less and less likely that he would get any answers. The raccoon was nowhere to be found. The bear checked Joe's Mug right after leaving the boardinghouse, but the moose only shook his heavy head. "Haven't seen him."

Young Joe Junior also shook his head, in an almost-perfect imitation of his father. "Lefty was rooting around the garbage in the back two days ago, in the morning. But yesterday and today . . . nothing."

Orville asked at the bank next. The bank employees hadn't seen him, and they always kept an eye out for Lefty.

Then he went to the newspaper office. The rabbit at the reception desk said he hadn't heard one way or another but would ask the reporters as they came in and send word to Orville immediately if anyone knew something.

Orville had the odd impression that the rabbit was chuckling as he turned to leave. He whirled around again. "Is the fox in?"

"Vera's out at the moment. But you could talk to Gladys Honeysuckle. She's really the one who knows everything in town."

Orville weighed the pitfalls of getting caught in a conversation with Gladys versus the chance that she might know something useful. He decided to risk it. He trooped over to Gladys's desk and put the question to her: "Any idea where Lefty might be, Ms. Honeysuckle?"

Gladys inhaled—always a dangerous sign. "Well, finally! I'm glad someone is taking the initiative in this town. That raccoon is up to his ears in illegal activity and the police never do anything about it. Well, if it's gone to murder, I say it's high time that criminal got arrested, if he's done it. Life just hasn't been the same since; I can barely sleep a wink at night, and it's just awful for the little ones in this town—we raised them right, we did, and now it's as bad as if we were living in the worst neighborhood in the worst city in the world, and what's the point of coming to a sweet town like this if murders are simply allowed to happen? I'm just telling you what I hear, Officer. I know you mean well and do your best in your way—bless your heart—but this is a problem that must be solved, and soon. You know that raccoon is involved! He must be. He's shifty. He leaves town for days on end. Off on some criminal enterprise, you may be sure—" She broke off to take a deep breath.

"Where?" Orville got out.

"I'm not privy to his nefarious doings! Somewhere outside town, though, because he hasn't been seen by anyone for days, not even a peep. He must have a hidey-hole somewhere. Some dank and horrible place, probably—"

"But you don't know where?" the bear pressed.

"No," Gladys said sourly, upset by this gap in her considerable knowledge. "But I'm sure he's hiding there now."

"I see. Thank you, Ms. Honeysuckle!"

Orville hurried away before the hummingbird could trap him in a longer conversation and continued his hunt. Having exhausted the obvious routes open to him, he chose to print up wanted signs for Lefty, which was easy, since the police department kept a mockup of Lefty's wanted poster at the ready.

Orville put the sign up in all the public buildings and made a formal announcement that Lefty was wanted by the police. Any beast who saw him was now obligated to tell the police where Lefty was, and assisting the fugitive was strictly forbidden.

The day passed without any sightings of Lefty, but the news of Orville's interest got around. Shady Hollow was buzzing with the gossip, and creatures assumed the bear had found some crucial piece of evidence to prove Lefty was the killer after all.

Neighbors shook their heads knowingly. Of course! It was the criminal element after all. No upstanding citizen of the Hollow could have done such a terrible deed.

Vera and Lenore heard the news while they were at the bookshop the next day.

The fox sighed. "I was worried this might happen. Orville is taking the easy way out. He won't search for the truth if he gets his paws on Lefty. He'll use the prints as evidence and say

Lefty is guilty of the whole thing. Lefty probably doesn't have an alibi, so he ran. He doesn't stand a chance."

"What makes you think Lefty is innocent?" Lenore asked, tipping her head sideways.

"I just feel it in my fur. He doesn't have a real reason for either murder. And he can barely rob a fruit stand without messing it up. How could he plan two murders successfully, with no witnesses at all?" Vera shook her head in disgust. "It just doesn't make sense."

"You'll have a hard time proving Lefty's innocence if you can't talk to him," said Lenore. "He's lucky there's anyone on his side at all. Most folks would just as soon see him put away for life."

"He might be a criminal, but he's not a murderer."

Wishing Lenore good night, Vera left the bookstore and started along the path to her den.

As Vera made her way, she heard a stick crack on the path behind her. She stopped and listened, her ears and her guard up. No creature could be too careful these days. Lucky for her, she had keen ears.

Then a hooded figure stepped out from behind a tree.

"Are you Vera Vixen, the reporter?" asked the unfamiliar animal. "I have to talk to you."

"You can make an appointment at the newsroom," Vera replied, walking a little faster.

"Please, Miss Vixen," the creature called after her. "I have to save my Lefty from the police. He didn't do anything wrong!"

Vera stopped in her tracks and spun around. "Your Lefty? Who are you, anyway?"

The stranger pulled off the hood. It was a raccoon. "I'm Rhonda," she said. "Lefty and I are together."

Vera's temporary fear dissolved as she sniffed a story. "It's nice to meet you, Rhonda. Why don't you let me buy you a cup of coffee?" Vera could always use a cup of coffee, and she knew Rhonda would be more forthcoming if they were sitting together and chatting like friends.

The two new acquaintances headed over to Joe's Mug. Vera was curious to hear what Rhonda had to say, but she kept her questions to herself until Rhonda was ensconced at a table with a large coffee and an even larger maple-nut scone.

"Where is Lefty?" Vera asked. "Don't worry, I'm not the police. I won't tell . . . if you actually turn out to be a source."

"I couldn't say," Rhonda hedged, looking sideways. "But I know he never killed anyone."

Rhonda told Vera a little about herself. To be perfectly honest, Rhonda was more than a little miffed that folks in Shady Hollow had no idea who she was. She couldn't believe Lefty had never mentioned her to his neighbors. After all, they had been together for a number of years.

"How did you know to come to Shady Hollow at all?" Vera asked.

Rhonda explained that word had gotten to her about the paw print found in the von Beaverpelt mansion and Orville's suspicion that Lefty might be guilty of more than theft.

"I love Lefty," Rhonda assured Vera, "but even I know he isn't the sharpest stick in the woods. He means well, but he doesn't always think things through, if you know what I mean."

Vera nodded, taking a sip of her rapidly cooling coffee. She did not want to interrupt Rhonda's flow of words, but she feared the raccoon would never get to the point. Rhonda seemed determined to tell Vera all the details of her and Lefty's star-crossed relationship, and Vera wanted no part of that. She was only interested in the facts.

"So what was Lefty doing in von Beaverpelt's house?" she asked sternly. "The police found a raccoon paw print, and there's no denying that."

"That was nothing." Rhonda sighed and then leaned in toward Vera like an old friend exchanging a secret. "It happened a long time ago, but the police never had call to dust for prints until now. Lefty was just looking around the mansion. Just curious, you see. He's not a murderer."

Vera may not have approved of Lefty's morals in general, but she had to agree with Rhonda—he was no murderer.

So who was?

Letting Rhonda spin on, Vera drifted into a daydream in which she was receiving a prestigious prize for her story on solving a murder in a small town. These pleasant thoughts were interrupted by Rhonda banging her empty coffee cup on the table.

Vera started and blinked, realizing she was still at Joe's with her new best friend.

Rhonda had understood that she was beginning to lose her audience and was struggling for more information to hold the fox's interest.

"Don't you want to hear about how Lefty and I met?" she ventured. "It's a great story. We were both casing the same house and—"

Vera broke in at this point. "I'm so sorry, but I'm on a deadline. I appreciate the information on Lefty, but I have to get back to the paper. Thanks so much for talking with me. If Lefty wants to talk, send a note to the paper with the code word *cranberry*. I'll go anywhere to meet him and get the story."

After Vera made her escape from the chatty raccoon, she decided to head home to peruse Otto's journals. She felt certain that there was a clue in them somewhere. She couldn't afford to waste any more time on Lefty's love life. She was positive that someone else had not only killed Otto Sumpf and Reginald von Beaverpelt but also tried to kill her, with the boulder in the woods. If only Vera could find out who before they made another attempt on her life!

Chapter 26

Vera made it safely to her den without encountering any other creature. She breathed a sigh of relief as she shut the heavy oak front door. After a moment's indecision, she threw the bolt of the brand-new shiny brass lock.

What a farce, she thought. Both Reginald and Otto were killed outside their homes. The new locks being sold weren't making the town safer at all.

But she didn't unlock the door.

Instead she turned to the table where Otto's journals were neatly stacked. It was high time to look through them carefully. Intending to do exactly that, Vera curled up on the couch with her reading glasses, Otto's journals, and some dried figs.

There were eight journals. Most of the entries were random

comments about his neighbors, rants about various topics, or descriptions of what he had for lunch. Vera read diligently, though, making little notes whenever something relevant popped out at her.

Hours later, she got up and paced back and forth in her living room to clear her brain. After several rotations, she noticed something she'd missed when first returning to her den: a folded slip of paper had been slid underneath the door. She pounced on it and unfolded it as fast as she could.

The writing was so jagged and scrawled that Vera had to read it through three times before she could understand the message: *Get off the von Beaverpelt case, fox. The next boulder won't miss.*

Vera was more perplexed than frightened by the threatening note. She was an investigative reporter; it would take far more than a warning to get her off the case. She examined the writing itself, trying to discern what sort of creature might have done it. But it was clear that, whoever it was, they'd disguised their own style by using this nearly illiterate jumble. She held the paper up to a lantern and squinted to see if any clues were visible that way.

In the light, a faint watermark appeared: the image of a large sycamore tree. Where had Vera seen that before?

She rummaged through her stack of papers. She knew she'd seen something very like the watermark not too long ago. Where was it?

Vera took a quick breath as she spied the same watermark on another piece of paper. With trembling paws, she pulled it out.

It was the invitation to Reginald von Beaverpelt's wake, written by none other than Edith von Beaverpelt.

Vera put the invitation down. If both papers came from the von Beaverpelt mansion—which seemed likely, because who else would be able to afford such high-quality paper?—it pointed to one thing. Edith had so recently told Vera that folk who got in her way regretted it.

So Edith must be the one who warned her off the case with this new note. And why would she do that unless she was the killer?

Vera was now as awake as if she'd drunk three cups of Joe's coffee. Whatever the writer of the note intended, the effect made Vera even more determined. She could look for clues related to Edith in Otto's writing. Perhaps Otto had seen or overheard something significant and that was why he was killed.

The fox examined the journals for a long time but didn't see any clues pointing to Edith. But there were plenty of sections she couldn't read.

"He wrote in another language for part of these," she muttered aloud. "Maybe Professor Heidegger can read it, or he may have an insight into these scribbles around the edge. It looks like Otto had a code of some sort. He used only initials for most of the creatures in town. He didn't want anyone to stumble on his diary, that's for sure."

He was a spy once, Vera remembered. He may have just gotten into the habit of hiding his work.

Vera resolved to talk to Heidegger right away. She had to venture into the darkness to find the nocturnal creature, but Vera was a fox, with sharp claws and sharper teeth. She wasn't afraid of the dark . . . or of what the dark might hide.

So she put the journals in her satchel and unlocked the

door. As she made her way through the woods, hurrying past shadow after shadow, she couldn't help but glance over her shoulder now and again. Any creature would be a bit nervous after the events of the past week, and Vera was getting awfully close to catching the killer.

When she arrived at Professor Heidegger's residence, Vera felt a jolt of relief. He was home, up on the high branch he used as his balcony.

"Professor!" she called. "Hello!"

As soon as Heidegger saw his visitor, he soared down to meet her. "How are you this fine evening, Miss Vixen?" asked the owl politely.

"As well as can be expected. Thank you for asking, Professor." Too nervous after her walk to indulge in more pleasantries, Vera rummaged in her bag for the two most recent of Otto's journals.

"I was really hoping you could help me understand these," Vera explained as she produced the diaries. "They're Otto's. Parts of them appear to be in some kind of code, or foreign language, or both."

She offered them to the owl, who looked them over with interest, his large eyes seeming to glow in the dim light.

"How fascinating! But I must have some privacy and some time to peruse these, Miss Vixen," the owl warned. "This is not a simple matter."

"Of course, Professor," Vera replied, although she had been hoping for a quick answer. "Will you please contact me if you learn anything?"

"You'll be hearing from me," the owl responded confidently. "I am gifted with many languages, and there is not a code that has ever been devised that Ambrosius Heidegger couldn't crack!"

Vera, drawing on all her inner strength, resisted the urge to make a catty remark and thanked the professor for his time and expertise.

Chapter 27

Vera got back to her den without any problem, and she locked the door as soon as she shut it. Her mind raced with possibilities. Otto's journals. The missing Lefty. Edith's special paper.

She barely slept, and the next morning came far too fast. She dragged herself to the newspaper office well after her usual time. At her desk, she dozed until a voice interrupted her slumber.

"Miss Vixen? Miss Vixen!"

"That's the lede!" she muttered, then blinked awake. "Huh? What?"

Vera looked up to see a rabbit holding a folded piece of paper. "This message came for you. Anonymous tip."

"Thanks." Vera reached for it. The note read: *For the best cranberry pie, go to Joe's Mug for the midnight special. Come alone—this pie is too good to share.*

Still groggy, Vera read the note over and over, trying to make sense of it. Joe's wasn't open at midnight . . . Wait—the note used the code word. Rhonda was a lot brighter than Lefty; she must have written the note. Vera was supposed to meet Rhonda outside Joe's at midnight tonight if she wanted to meet with Lefty! The fox was excited, and even though the note warned her to come alone, she intended to tell Lenore where she was going. She had learned her lesson about secret midnight meetings.

When Vera went over to the bookstore and told the raven what she planned to do, her friend said, "Are you sure? Think of what happened the last time you met someone based on a note! Why not ask Orville to follow along?"

Vera shook her head. "It would never work. I think raccoons can smell police from fifty paces."

"Well, what if I just sort of hovered around the scene?"

"That's more what I had in mind."

Lenore would fly to Joe's from the bookshop, and Vera would go from her den just in case she was being watched.

Vera spent the rest of the day trying to work but too distracted to get much done. She headed to her den early and finally fell into an exhausted sleep after eating a little dinner.

She woke up with a start, though she had no idea what made her do so. Blinking, Vera looked at the clock. "Oh, it's quarter to! I have to go!"

She dashed to Joe's Mug, arriving there just before midnight.

She knew Lenore was there, too, watching from above.

The fox paced up and down in front of the store, waiting for Rhonda or Lefty to show. After a few minutes, she heard a hiss from the shadows.

"*Pssst.* Hey, fox. Come over here."

Vera was nervous, but she knew this might be her only chance to get a vital clue. She edged over into the shadows. Rhonda was there, dressed in a dark trench coat. The markings across her eyes made her look extremely sinister.

"Follow me if you want to talk to Lefty," said Rhonda. She barely waited for Vera's assent before starting to hurry away into the woods.

"Where are we going?" Vera asked as she ran along beside the raccoon. "Is Lefty close by?"

"He's in a safe place" was the only thing Rhonda would say.

The fox kept following the raccoon deeper into the woods. It was soon obvious that Lefty was nowhere within Shady Hollow.

After what seemed like hours, the raccoon and the fox reached a small settlement that Rhonda announced as Elm Grove. This was where she made her home and where she had been hiding Lefty from Shady Hollow police and anyone else who might have been after him.

They arrived at a tidy little cottage tucked by the river. It was covered in morning glory vines and had neat vegetable patches on either side of the front yard. Vera hoped Lenore was still flying silently above.

Rhonda unlocked the front door and invited Vera in. Vera was unsurprised to see Lefty in the living room.

He jumped nervously when Vera entered. "Oh, it's you!" he said.

"Of course it's me. You asked me to come."

Lefty nodded. "I did, I did. Were you followed?"

Rhonda looked annoyed. "Of course we weren't followed! I know how to cover tracks!"

Vera was all business. She whipped out her reporter's notebook and sat down on the upholstered chair closest to Lefty. "I've got a few questions for you," she began.

Lefty looked at Vera fearfully. "I didn't do it, fox!"

"I believe you."

That wasn't something Lefty was used to hearing. "You do? You'll tell the bear that, won't you?"

"Of course I will, Lefty. In fact, I've already told him. But what we need is to ferret out the real killer," Vera replied. "If we can prove who killed Otto and Reginald, then you're off the hook . . . at least, as far as the murder goes." She knew Lefty was up to his ears in other criminal activities. Jewel thefts, black market honey . . . "I don't know Orville that well, but I trust him to be honest."

Both Rhonda and Lefty looked relieved at this pronouncement. Lefty, though, was still looking nervous, as if he expected Orville to show up at the door at any minute.

"What do you want to know from me?"

"First, what were you doing in the von Beaverpelt mansion? Your paw print was found when Orville dusted."

Lefty shrugged. "That doesn't have anything to do with it!" He reiterated what Rhonda had said to Vera at Joe's. Lefty had been casing the joint about a month ago, but he hadn't gotten far when he had to turn tail and run to avoid being discovered.

"But I haven't been there since," he protested. "I had a good gig with, um, a client. It seemed pretty close to legal, too! All I had to do was pay cash to buy jewels."

"Who were you working for?"

Lefty shook his head. "Ain't saying. I learned my lesson. No more odd jobs! Not for jewels, not for delivering plum wine . . ."

"You did drop it off, then." Vera smelled the story in Lefty's words. "Tell me what happened."

"I can't say." The raccoon looked terrified. "But the wine tipped me off. I just thought I was doing a little job for some beast—I swear I didn't know it was poisoned! I was told to leave it by the pond, and I did."

"Told by who?"

Lefty shut his trap and shook his head violently. "No way, fox. I'll end up dead, too, if I tell anyone."

"He won't even tell me," Rhonda said.

"You have to come clean, Lefty," Vera told the raccoon firmly. "Your real problem is with Orville. He wants to arrest you for the murder of Reginald von Beaverpelt. Sooner or later, he is going to find you."

"I'll run if I have to," Lefty said.

"No!" Rhonda interrupted. "If you run, everyone will always call you a murderer. You won't be safe anywhere."

"But . . ."

Vera stood up. "Look, Lefty. I can't force you to tell the truth. But if you come back to Shady Hollow, you'll be an important witness. Orville won't hurt you . . . he'll protect you from whoever is scaring you." She walked to the door. "Think about it, raccoon. You'll go from being a criminal to a hero. Don't you want that?"

Lefty sighed as he shook his head. "Nope. I want to live."

Chapter 28

It was a long walk back to Shady Hollow. Vera was stumbling with exhaustion by the time she reached her den, and even Lenore was winded from the hours of low-level flying.

"Get some sleep," the raven advised. "You're no good to anyone if you can't think! See you later."

Vera slept like the dead. When she awoke, it was after noon. She hurried to the newspaper office to write up another column. BW was pacing madly on his desk, shouting at everyone to get to work.

Vera sweated over her notes. What did she have? Nothing she felt she could print. Only Ruby's comments about the affair, and that fancy paper she'd traced back to the von Beaverpelt mansion. She had gone over her conversation at the cemetery with Ruby again and again. Yet she simply could not write an article featuring Ruby's accusations against Edith, not even with the threatening note or the interview she'd had with Edith that ended so awkwardly. It wasn't enough. The newspaper dealt in facts, and the dedicated reporter was having a hard time figuring which of her many facts were the important ones. Something was not quite right.

Despite BW's urgings to stay and write, Vera left for her den. "I can't think in here, BW, and it's close to quitting time anyway."

"You're a reporter, Vixen! You need to think in a place like this! The clackity noise is key!"

"See you tomorrow, BW," she called.

When she arrived home, Vera found Professor Heidegger waiting for her.

"I found something that may interest you," he said.

Vera invited him inside, and they sat at the table after she made some peppermint tea.

"As you guessed, the toad wrote his personal diaries in a combination of languages, with a fairly common cryptic code pattern thrown in for good measure," the owl explained. "Fortunately, I have made a study of such things."

Professor Heidegger was certain that Otto did this more to amuse himself than to hide the content. The first of the two journals was not terribly interesting, mainly a list of what the toad had to eat every day and his plans for the evenings, which consisted mostly of drinking wine and grousing about the state of the world.

The owl tossed that journal aside in favor of the other one. "This journal is far more intriguing. It's full of Otto's dealings with his neighbors in Shady Hollow. Arguments with von Beaverpelt over use of the millpond, suspicions of Sun Li and what he actually puts in his vegetable stir-fry, and a dispute with Lenore over the condition of some used novels. The toad seemed to have a bone to pick with everyone."

"Well, that's no secret," Vera said. "I don't suppose you found anything about Mrs. von Beaverpelt?"

"Not directly," Professor Heidegger said. "Otto Sumpf and Ruby Ewing were friends, better friends than she's ever let on. Otto detailed in his diary how Ruby often came to visit him and talk about her problems. The unlikely pair both felt like outcasts in the town, although for very different reasons. Otto was exactly the sort of contrarian who would associate with Ruby just for the notoriety. The toad would complain about the latest grievance committed against him by a neighbor, and Ruby would share how she had been snubbed by the proprietor of the grocery store."

Professor Heidegger was skimming through the pages that chronicled Otto and Ruby's friendship. "Here," he said. "The name of Reginald von Beaverpelt. It seems Ruby confided in Otto about her affaires de coeur. As we know from the wake, Ruby had been having an affair with Reginald von Beaverpelt, and she suspected Mrs. von Beaverpelt was aware of it."

"Yes, she confirmed that to me later, at the cemetery. Go on."

"According to Otto's jottings, Ruby was deeply in love with the married beaver, and she wanted them to run away together. When von Beaverpelt refused and broke things off with her, she retaliated by blackmailing him. She threatened to expose their affair not only to Edith and her daughters but to the entire town of Shady Hollow."

Vera nodded slowly. "That fits! Chitters knew money was

going missing at the sawmill, paid to a B. S.: *Blackmailing Sheep*! Von Beaverpelt would lose his position of respect in the town, so he had to pay her off. But then he grew angry and resentful. No matter what Ruby thought, he would never leave Edith. She was the one in the marriage with all the money, and she controlled the purse strings. So she had a stake in keeping things quiet, too."

The owl continued sipping tea. "This journal is evidence. It proves that Ruby Ewing was blackmailing von Beaverpelt."

"How does that help prove murder?" Vera asked. "Blackmailers tend to *not* want to murder their victims. If they do, the money dries up. Even if we have a blackmailer, the murderer gets away."

"Perhaps there's another clue you can use." Not normally one for strong emotion, the professor was fluffing his feathers and hopping around Vera's living room in agitation. "Here's the passage in which Ruby tells Otto she has an insurance policy hidden in the woods, in a hollow log. She told Otto, 'It's so me,' but he doesn't explain what that means. There must be a clue there. Orville might be able to investigate."

Not Orville! Vera thought. *She* would discover the link.

"Thank you for bringing these over. I'll take it to the police," Vera said, keeping her thoughts to herself.

Heidegger left and Vera paced. *It's so me.* That phrase was familiar. Where had she heard it before? What was the truth? Did Edith find out about the affair and kill Reginald in anger, as Ruby claimed? And what insurance policy could the sheep have? She didn't make much money at Goody Crow's . . . Vera stopped short.

Of course. The blackmail money. It was too much money

for one creature to hide, unless it was converted into something small and valuable. Something that might fit in a hollow log.

"*It's so me,*" she breathed. "Rubies!"

What else could it be? Ruby must have hired Lefty to conduct the shady business of buying up rubies with her blackmail payments. He was known to steal and fence jewels, and he'd said he'd been doing that kind of gig. But as soon as Lefty became a suspect in two murders, he'd disappeared, too scared to deal with the police. Now Vera might be the only creature in town besides Ruby who knew where the secret stash from von Beaverpelt's blackmail money could be. With it, Vera could force Ruby to tell her what she knew about the affair and maybe discover the evidence that would finally prove Edith guilty of murder.

Vera peeked outside. Deep billowing clouds had amassed on the western horizon, stealing the very last light of day from the sky. A storm was coming. If Vera was quick, she might find the evidence before she got drenched.

She ran into the woods, toward the hollow log mentioned in the diary. She knew which log it was. For a reporter like Vera, it was important to know all the interesting places around the forest. She reached the clearing. In the fading light, she saw the distinctive hollow birch log that could be hiding the evidence. She bent down and put a paw carefully inside, feeling for any foreign object.

Behind her, a twig snapped.

"Always sticking your pretty snout where it doesn't belong. So you didn't heed my note after all. Turn around, fox."

Vera turned around slowly to face the voice. The voice of the murderer.

The voice of Ruby Ewing.

Chapter 29

ome along, Vera," Ruby said. "You don't have much of a choice." To emphasize her point, Ruby held up a knife.

Vera stared at the knife gleaming dully in the night. A flash of lightning suddenly made the blade glitter. Without really knowing what she was doing, Vera backed up a few steps.

Ruby closed the distance between them, her eyes calm and cool. "Keep going, Vixen. We've got a bit of a walk."

"Where are we going?"

"High Cliff. There's a cottage up there. It's going to be your new home for a while."

"What are you going to do?"

"I'm leaving this place, and I can't have you free to set the cops on me. You'll get out okay if you just follow my orders."

Ruby sounded so resigned, so ordinary, as if they were working out the details of a surprise party.

With no other option, Vera allowed Ruby to direct her through the blustery and dark forest to High Cliff. The wind tossed the leaves wildly, ripping some from their branches and sending them spiraling between the trees in a green haze. The lightning flashed ever more frequently, and the thunder grew louder as the storm approached. The air lay heavy, making it hard to breathe.

It was a long way to High Cliff, and Ruby kept a brutal pace; Vera couldn't tell whether she was merely trying to beat the storm or if she had another reason to hurry.

Fat drops of rain began to hit the ground long before the creatures started climbing the swiftly rising ground at the base of High Cliff. Vera stumbled, and Ruby's knife jabbed into her leg.

"No slipups, fox. You're doing fine."

The sheep was vigilant; there was no way Vera would be able to escape without a major distraction. Oh, why hadn't she told Lenore what she was up to? Or anyone? The impending dark, the storm, and the pursuit of the story had made her rush against her better judgment. Now she was paying the price for that stupid decision. The sheep was leading her ever farther from help. Despite Ruby's assurance, Vera wondered if she'd get out of High Cliff alive.

High Cliff was a secluded spot, even by forest standards. It sat at the very top of a long ridge that rolled down to the river. In clear weather, the view was spectacular. But the climb was not for the faint of heart. It was practically a mountain, with rough ground, a thin trail, and frequent outcroppings of ancient timeworn boulders on each side of the path.

Vera hurried as fast as she dared, for Ruby wasn't shy with the knife and she never let the pace slacken. The raindrops began to hit harder, becoming a sheet of water. Vera was soaked to the bone by the time she stumbled onto the flat top of the ridge, her red fur slick and matted. They had climbed the only accessible side. On the other, the land fell away sharply to the riverbank—the name High Cliff was perfectly appropriate.

Ruby gave the panting fox a little kick with her hooves. "Move it, fox. Over to the cottage."

Dimly, Vera saw what Ruby was referencing. Through the rain, she could see the outline of a small cottage. The thatched roof came down so low that the windows were mostly concealed. Even the door was set low. Ruby forced Vera over to the door and made her open it, shoving the fox to the floor before she followed inside.

Vera heard the heavy bang of the old door being barred and then the strike of a match. Vera was so tired that Ruby had a lantern lit before she could rise and face her kidnapper.

Ruby Ewing stood there, surprisingly dry and dangerously calm. She gazed at Vera with an expression of pity.

"You stupid, stupid animal. I warned you to forget about the story. But you had to keep hounding me. This is your fault, really. You deserve what you get."

"How can you say that when you are the beast who killed both Otto and Reginald?"

"Reginald deserved it, too," Ruby said, her tone heating up at last. "He used me. I loved him, and he was going to throw me aside, just to maintain appearances."

"You are no innocent in this, Ruby. You were blackmailing him."

"So what if I was? He could afford it. He wanted the rich life and a little something on the side. Why shouldn't I make him pay for it? If he hadn't been such a stuffed shirt, we could have just run off and made a new life somewhere else. But he was beholden to his shrew of a wife. He couldn't turn down her money!" Ruby was gesturing wildly with the knife.

"So you killed him." Vera took a few careful steps back, deeper into the cottage, away from the blade.

"He was going to talk," said the sheep. "He was going to go to the press. To the police!"

"So you tried to poison him with the plum wine."

"Reggie was cheap. He never turned down anything he could find free. I thought I'd put a bottle of wine in his path—he never varied his path to the sawmill. I figured he'd grab it, thinking he saved a few cents, and drink it. No more problems. I didn't want to be seen with the bottle, so I hired Lefty to leave it by the pond. But the raccoon left it in the wrong spot—Otto found it instead. When Lefty told me where he left it, I got so mad, I almost killed him right there. I should have. Instead I went to find Otto, hoping to steal the bottle back before he drank it. But it was too late. I found him lying on the edge of the pond, dead.

"Well, I couldn't let anyone know there was poison in the wine bottle. Lefty would hear about Otto and figure it out and then spill everything! So I found a knife and stabbed Otto to make it look like he died another way."

"It was your one mistake," said Vera, putting the pieces together. "If you'd just pushed him out into the pond, the police wouldn't have guessed murder. Otto wasn't young. They would have assumed it was from heart failure or a night of heavy drinking and an accidental drowning. It was the knife that brought in the medical examiner who discovered the poison. And all for nothing. Otto never did a thing to you."

"It was a mistake," Ruby admitted. "I never wanted to hurt Otto. And I should never have trusted Lefty with anything. You want something done right, do it yourself! But the damage was done, and my original problem hadn't gone away. Reggie was still trying to ruin me."

"So you tried to poison him at his office."

The sheep nodded. "I had a key because we met there at night quite often. His wife thought he was working late. It was a little risky, but I snuck in one night and put the poison in his favorite coffeepot. He always used that one. But he didn't drink enough."

"And then von Beaverpelt knew you were after him," Vera guessed. "He passed me a message saying he wanted to talk after he nearly threw me out of his office the day before."

"He was going to tell you everything about me," Ruby said. "So I had to get him out of the picture. Pretending to be Howard, I sent a note to his mansion. Then I followed him. I thought I could convince him one last time to come with me. We could have vanished right then. I had the money hidden; we could have been happy.

"But he was scared. He wouldn't let me talk or explain anything." The sheep's eyes were red with unshed tears. "I pushed him. He was still weak from the poison, and he fell and hit his head on a rock, then slid into the water."

"You held him under," Vera accused.

"No!" said Ruby in protest. "I just . . . didn't help him out. He kept flailing around, yelping like a cub. It was pathetic, really. I was afraid someone would hear him and come running, but it didn't take long for him to drown. *Then* I pushed him down so the body wouldn't float up too soon and give it away."

"And then you went to work at the rest home as if it was an ordinary day. You slipped in like you had been there the whole time." Vera began to get truly scared when she realized how calculating Ruby was.

"It was easy." The sheep gave a little shrug. "No one in this town is too bright. Except maybe you, Vixen." Ruby focused on her again. "So you see why I can't let you leave."

Vera knew her time was running out. She thought frantically of a question to distract the sheep. "Why didn't you run right then, after killing him?"

"Yes, I suppose that would have been best. But I'm a bit of a gambler. I wondered if anyone would ever be able to connect me with the murders. By then Lefty had figured out that his errand had something to do with Otto's death. But Orville was convinced Lefty was guilty by that point, so I figured his leaving town was as good as me getting him out of the way."

"You would have let Lefty hang for your crime."

"He's a criminal anyway!"

"But he never *killed* anyone. You did! You even tried to kill me—in the woods with that boulder."

"You were too inquisitive. I didn't like it. Why can't folks just leave me in peace?"

"Maybe because you can't leave them in peace!" Vera burst out. "You never intended to let me live, did you, Ruby?"

"You know too much. You have a lot of friends in this town, fox. More than me, that's for sure. Once they realize you're missing, they'll come looking for you. I don't think it will take more than a week for them to find your body. By then I'll have retrieved my treasure and will be long gone!"

"Everyone will know you're the killer then." Vera jumped aside as Ruby made a grab for her.

"What do I care? Everyone in this town hates me because of how I choose to live my life. They won't be able to find me after I've gone, so let them gossip. It's what they're best at anyway."

"So why drag me all the way here? You could have escaped tonight, without all this."

"Reggie and I used to meet here sometimes when we were in love. It seemed like a good place to end it all. What can I say? I'm sentimental at heart."

"You're insane."

Ruby shook her head. "It'd be easier for you to believe that, wouldn't it? 'Crazy Ruby, driven to madness by her obsessions with love and money.' That's what they'll say in the end, anyway. But the truth is that I thought about each step and took it with my eyes open, because I wasn't afraid of the consequences. Murder isn't scary because it's crazy; it's scary because it's permanent."

She gave Vera a sad look. "That's why I warned you off the case. I didn't want to do something permanent to you."

Ruby lunged for Vera again, but the fox edged out of the way in time. The creatures scuffled across the floor of the cottage, kicking over tables and shoving chairs. Ruby brought the knife down and caught Vera's ear.

The fox howled so loudly that Ruby instinctively covered her ears, dropping the knife. Vera scrambled away, knocking over the lantern. Everything went pitch-black, with only strobe-like flashes of lightning entering through the little windows. Vera tried to get to the door, hoping to find and lift the bar out of the way so she could escape.

A scrape of metal behind her warned Vera that Ruby had found the knife. Feeling a presence behind her, she whirled away just as Ruby rammed the door with her head. Vera knew her only chance of escape was a window. Preparing to spring, she bunched herself up and leaped directly at the glass.

She squeezed her eyes shut and felt a hundred little cuts as the glass shattered around her. She hit the ground rolling and tried to ignore the sudden pain. Glass was embedded in her fur and skin. Ruby had unbarred the door by then and came charging out.

"Don't you dare, fox!" she yelled, preparing to run Vera down.

The fox caught a glimpse of a strange sight just then. Down the hill, a dozen flickering lights were coming through the trees. Lightning flashed, illuminating a number of dark shapes heading toward the cottage. Vera's heart soared for a moment. Help was coming!

Vera heard Ruby growl and hiss as she also took in the sight, and her heart fell again. It would be too late. The sheep was only a few feet from her.

Vera tried to roll away as Ruby attacked her, but the pain from jumping through the window was making her woozy. The knife connected with her paw and bit deep. Vera yelped. She mustered the energy to deflect the next blow, but Ruby seemed unstoppable.

The sheep raised her knife again, and Vera rolled once more, toward the cliffside. Ruby followed, aiming for Vera's heart. The sheep charged again, and Vera wondered if she could trick her into giving up. The fox moved back and feinted to the left just as Ruby pounced.

The grass was slick with rain. As Vera dodged out of the

way, Ruby couldn't stop her charge and bleated in alarm as she skidded toward the edge of the cliff.

Vera made an instinctive grab and caught Ruby's front leg just as she sailed over the edge. "Hold on!" Vera yelled.

But Ruby only kicked at the air and thrashed around, trying to wiggle free of Vera's grip. "Get away from me, fox. Let me go! I don't need anyone's help. Let me go!"

Ruby jerked her leg free of Vera's paw.

"No!" the fox shouted.

Ruby grinned triumphantly for just a second as she seemed to hover in empty space. Then, screaming, she plunged down toward the depths of the river far below.

Vera watched in horror as Ruby disappeared into the darkness. She continued lying there, her front paw dangling over the cliff edge. She panted, trying to regain her breath. She was in no shape to get down the hill on her own.

She closed her eyes, wondering if the rain was going to stop. Her body ached, and every time she moved, she felt glass jabbing into her. It was all so very tiring. Vera breathed in and out, starting to dream a little bit. She thought she heard Lenore's voice far away, and Orville's, and perhaps Joe's and Sun Li's. But she couldn't raise her head. The rain pattered over her as she lost consciousness.

Chapter 30

The storm raged at full force. Driving rain pelted down among the citizens of Shady Hollow as they raced to the top of the tall cliff. There they found the brave reporter—nearly unconscious, sopping wet, and cut up all over. The panda examined her carefully and then checked her pulse. He assured the anxious townsfolk gathered around that she would live but that they must stand back.

Vera's eyes fluttered open. "Ruby . . . went over the side."

"We'll find her," a deep voice growled. Orville was nearby, his expression either angry or concerned. "Or what's left of her."

"We'll look," Lenore said, gesturing for Gladys and Heidegger to join her. The birds flew over the edge of the cliff and down to the rocks below, where they discovered Ruby's broken body. She was beyond all help or censure now. Lenore said a little woodland prayer for the soul of Ruby Ewing.

Above, Vera had closed her eyes again.

"Please, we should hurry," Sun Li said in his quiet voice. "The fox must get medical care as soon as possible."

"Got it," Orville said. He picked Vera up and, once more, carried her back to the Hollow.

When Vera finally stirred and opened her eyes, the first thing she saw was Sun Li waiting patiently by her bedside. She was back in her own den. Sun Li had carefully cleaned and bandaged her many cuts and abrasions. Most of them were superficial, with the exception of a deep slice in the pad of her left forepaw. As Vera remembered what happened, she grew agitated.

The panda shushed her and told her to remain calm.

"You're safe," he assured her in a soothing tone. "The sheep is dead, and you're going to be fine." He hesitated for a moment and then continued. "You put yourself in danger for a newspaper story," Sun Li chided. "Maybe next time you will ask for help from another. You don't always have to do everything alone."

Vera didn't answer that but looked at her bandaged paw. "You're a pretty good doctor, Sun Li. And the Hollow could use a resident physician. Maybe it's time for a career change."

The panda smiled. "But who will cook for my regular customers? Get some rest, Miss Vixen. You won't heal if you don't sleep."

Vera nodded weakly as tears filled her eyes. She turned her face to the wall. She was much too feeble to deal with anything just yet. The panda patted her good paw with his own and left.

The next time Vera woke, she was pleased to see Lenore

sitting at her bedside. Lenore gently told her about finding Ruby's body. Sensing that her friend was not quite ready to talk about what happened with Ruby in those final desperate moments on High Cliff, Lenore instead told the story of how Professor Heidegger spotted Vera and Ruby traveling through the woods before the storm. He knew something about the scene was wrong and flew to Joe's Mug—the nearest place that was open—to find help.

"I'll have to thank the professor when I see him, using the biggest words possible," Vera said.

"This is the second time this week that you were almost killed," said Lenore. "I can't take this kind of stress. My feathers are starting to fall out."

Vera smiled at her friend and thought about what a close call she'd had. She was truly lucky to be alive. She found it hard to believe that Ruby was really dead and that all the drama and mystery was over. She would have to write an exclusive for the paper, but after that she was done. She wanted to put the whole awful experience behind her. The fox drifted off to sleep again as Lenore whispered good night.

The next day she felt well enough to sit up and start writing some notes for her article. Lenore had stayed at Vera's as a self-appointed nurse and guardian. Many creatures wanted to see Vera, but the raven turned most of them away. BW Stone was the hardest to control. The skunk threatened to spray Lenore and shouted to Vera from outside.

"Remember, fox, you work for me! Deadline is tomorrow at noon! Don't leave out any details! We're printing a double run!"

Vera listened from the safety of her den and laughed a bit but didn't respond.

"Vixen?" BW shouted. "Are you in there?"

"Shady Hollow has a noise ordinance, Stone," a new voice growled. "Do you want to write your editorial from a jail cell?"

"Sure," BW responded, undaunted. "That would boost sales!"

"*Clear off!*" Orville roared, likely violating the same noise ordinance he was claiming to uphold.

Vera knew Lenore would let Orville inside. No one said no to the police. And Orville had carried Vera all the way home. Twice.

The fox peeked in the mirror, nervously patting her fur into place. Bandages covered most of her, so it was a losing battle.

"Vera?" Lenore poked her head in the doorway. "Orville's come around."

"Yes, of course," Vera called, keeping her voice nonchalant. "Send him in."

Orville shuffled in, looking less confident than he'd sounded a moment ago. He carried a bouquet of flowers.

"Are those daisies?" Vera asked.

"I think so," the bear said. "They're for you." He held them out to her rather bashfully.

"Oh! Thank you!" Vera blushed. No one had given her flowers for a very long time. "That's, um . . . very kind. I love daisies."

He shuffled his paws. "Well, you did catch a murderer and all that. It was good work. And very brave."

"Thank you," she said again. To be called brave by a bear was high praise indeed.

Orville's eyes narrowed. "Though it was dangerous to go alone. You should have informed somebody."

"Believe me," Vera said, holding up her damaged paw, "I learned my lesson."

Orville sat down heavily in the chair next to Vera. He got ready to take careful notes for the official report. Vera told him of the notebooks and of the watermarked paper that she originally thought proved Edith's guilt. "Though it was purely circumstantial—the paper could have been stolen, or Edith might not have been the only one to use it."

Then she told him about the discovery of Ruby's blackmail and what led her to the woods in the hopes of finding the stash. Finally the fox relayed the story of how Ruby caught up with her in the woods and forced her at knifepoint out to High Cliff and the lonely cottage.

She told the bear what Ruby told her, word for word, about her relationship with von Beaverpelt, the accidental poisoning of Otto, the deliberate stabbing of Otto's body, and the drowning of von Beaverpelt. Vera's voice quivered somewhat as she relived the terrible battle in the cottage. She started to tear up as she told Orville how Ruby slipped in the mud and skidded over the cliff.

"I tried to save her," Vera insisted through her tears. "But she wouldn't let me."

Orville closed his notebook, clearly deciding that the witness had had enough for the time being. "It's not your fault, Vera."

"Isn't it? Isn't the whole thing all our fault, at least a little? Ruby had almost no one to talk to. She was treated badly by the whole town."

"No excuse for murder." Orville snorted. "Civilized creatures don't do that sort of thing."

Remembering she had important evidence, Vera offered Otto's journals to Orville.

"You withheld evidence from the police again! That's a violation."

"You're quite aware of the statutes all of a sudden."

"Well," Orville explained, "the chief is none too thrilled with the events of the past week and is already making noises about retiring so he can fish full-time. I think I might be running for chief soon, which means I ought to know the rules. So I've been studying up on the *Big Book of Policing*."

"That would be a refreshing change," she said. "An informed constabulary! I'd like to hear more about that plan."

"Well," Orville said nervously, "perhaps I could tell you more over dinner . . . when you're feeling better, of course."

Vera blushed to the tips of her ears. Daisies, and then an invitation to dinner? "I think I'd like that," she said.

"Oh, really? Well. Um. Good!" Orville grinned foolishly. "Then feel better. I have to, um, go policing now."

"I'll see you soon," she promised.

Epilogue

Vera recovered remarkably fast. After all, the story had to be written. No rest for the reporter! She penned her article as quickly as she could. The next day the *Herald*'s rabbits carried her written version of the encounter at High Cliff to the newspaper offices with all due speed, to be published in a special edition very soon.

Later that same day, Esmeralda von Beaverpelt knocked on her door.

"Would you mind coming to the sawmill, Miss Vixen? Mama's there, and she asked for you especially."

Vera sniffed a scoop, so she followed Esme there.

Edith von Beaverpelt was pacing around Reginald's old

office. When she saw Vera, she nodded curtly. "Miss Vixen. You look terrible."

"Thank you, ma'am," Vera said. "Before we get started, I have a quick question for you." She held out both pieces of the fine watermarked paper, which she'd brought along. "This first one is the invitation to your husband's funeral; the other is a threat delivered to me. Do you know how Ruby might have got ahold of your paper?"

Edith looked at both pieces of paper. "Oh, my. Yes. I donated a number of items to Goody Crow's a few months ago—including a ream of the sycamore paper. She must have found it there."

"That explains it, then," Vera said. So it was just chance, working in Ruby's favor again.

Edith nodded and then ordered her secretary, "Bring Chitters in."

"What's this meeting about?" Vera asked.

"Just have your notebook ready," Edith said.

Howard arrived and hovered nervously in the doorway. He wrung his paws until Edith looked up and saw him there.

"Oh, for pity's sake, Howard," she said. "Come in and sit down. I'm not going to eat you."

Howard looked terrified that he was about to lose his job. "Yes, boss?" he squeaked.

"It has come to my attention," Edith began in a formal tone, "that you do very fine work here at the mill. You got it up and running again when I asked you to, and everyone approves of your management. I would like to offer you a promotion. I want you to be sawmill director, effective immediately. I will remain chair of the board and will make all the crucial financial decisions, but I want you to be in charge of the mill's day-to-day operations. What do you say, Chitters?"

Howard was speechless for about a minute, but, not being a fool, he recovered and nodded his head.

"Thank you, Mrs. von Beaverpelt," he managed to get out. "I would be happy to accept the position of sawmill director." He straightened up and tried to look like a captain of industry.

Vera grinned widely and winked at Howard before she started scribbling in her notebook. "I'll have a few questions for you both," she said. The fox was impressed with Edith's move. The widow knew that Shady Hollow needed good news after so much tragedy. This would be the perfect story.

The next day, Vera scanned a fresh copy of that day's edition of the Shady Hollow *Herald*.

Right above the fold was the main headline:

PASSION AND POISON

THE COMPLETE CONFESSION
OF RUBY EWING

by Vera Vixen, staff reporter

THE STORY THAT HELD THE TOWN OF SHADY HOLLOW IN ITS GRIP FOR WEEKS HAS FINALLY COME TO AN END, A TRAGEDY THAT SEEMED TO END A STRING OF TRAGEDIES, SOME ACCIDENTAL AND OTHERS ALL TOO CALCULATED. RUBY EWING, HAVING CONFESSED TO THE MURDERS OF OTTO SUMPF AND REGINALD VON BEAVERPELT, MAKES A CONVINCING VILLAINESS. BUT HER STORY HOLDS

SADNESS, TOO. SHE CONDEMNED THE SOCIETY THAT
JUDGED HER EVEN AS SHE CRAVED ITS APPROVAL . . .

But on the side column, there was another note:

CHITTERS STEPS UP; VON B REMAINS ON BOARD

Mrs. von B Declares "Complete Confidence" in Mouse

FOR FULL STORY, SEE *Business, B1*

Vera read over both stories and smiled, a little sadly. Big
news for a small town. She hoped her days would soon be back
to normal.

"When's the next spelling bee?" she asked one of the staff
rabbits.

"Fourth of next month! My son's going to be in the middle-
grade round!" the rabbit said.

"Mark it down as my story!" Vera said. "I can't wait to
cover it."

"Yes, Miss Vixen." The rabbit looked her over more carefully. "Say, you look nice today. Very polished."

"Oh, really?" Vera asked, looking over her new outfit. "I
don't look like I'm trying too hard, do I?"

"Too hard for what?"

Another rabbit ran in then. "Miss Vixen, Deputy Orville is
here. He says you have a date—that is, an interview! Yes, he
says you have an interview!"

"Thank you! I'll be right down."

Vera grabbed her bag and leveled a dark look at both rabbits. "Not one word to that gossip-columnist hummingbird. Understand?"

Both creatures nodded vigorously, their ears flapping. "Oh, yes. Not a problem. Wouldn't dream of it."

"Good." Vera dashed downstairs, where a certain polished-looking bear waited.

The rabbits watched her go, then looked at each other. "Race you to Gladys's desk?" asked one.

"On your mark . . . get set . . . *go!*"

The End

Acknowledgments

Between us, we have constructed a world of woodland creatures who live, work, and murder in a delightful small community. But the creation of the Shady Hollow Mystery series was most definitely a group effort.

At the outset, Nicholas Tulach served as our first publisher at Hammer & Birch, going above and beyond to get our stories into book form and out into the world.

We are eternally grateful to our former boss and current friend Daniel Goldin, owner and proprietor of Boswell Book Company in Milwaukee, Wisconsin. He was one of our first readers and a tireless cheerleader for the books, hand selling them to anyone who crossed his path and stood still long enough. May all authors be so lucky.

We would also like to thank our friends and family who bought the books, attended our events, and were kind enough to tell us how much they enjoyed the stories. This love and encouragement kept us writing and helped us explore the world of Shady Hollow, allowing us to discover new characters and places in every book.

Many thanks go to Jason Gobble, publishing rep extraordinaire, for being awesome. We can never thank you enough for your generous support of these books in particular and for being a champion of books in general.

And we must thank Caitlin Landuyt, editor at Vintage Books & Anchor Books, who gave these mysteries a fresh launch into the world and fulfilled dreams we didn't even know we had.

Additionally, Sharon would like to say: Thank you to my beloved husband, Mark, who believes in me and supports me in everything I do.

And Jocelyn says: A huge thanks to my parents, who raised me on PBS murder mysteries, taught me to love reading, and didn't flinch when I chose to major in English. These books are for you.

And thank you, Nick, for always being there. You are without doubt the best thing to happen to me, and I love you more than cheese.

Read more from
Juneau Black

The Shady Hollow
Mystery Series

"A cross between *Twin Peaks*
and *Fantastic Mr. Fox*."
—Milwaukee Record

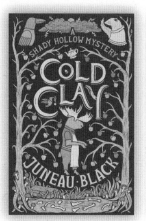